BEST
GAY EROTICA
2011

BEST
GAY EROTICA
2011

Series Editor
RICHARD LABONTÉ

Selected and Introduced by
KEVIN KILLIAN

CLEIS
PRESS

Published in the United States by Cleis Press Inc.,
2246 Sixth Street, Berkeley, California 94710.

Printed in the United States.
Cover design: Scott Idleman
Cover photograph: Pixtal Images
Text design: Frank Wiedemann
Cleis logo art: Juana Alicia
First Edition.
10 9 8 7 6 5 4 3 2 1

ISBN: 978-1-57344-424-8

"I Dreamt" © 2010 by Shane Allison. "Beauty #2" © 2009 by Eric Karl Anderson, reprinted with the author's permission from *Ganymede Stories One*, edited by John Stahle, first appeared in *Ganymede* #6 (January 2010). "Shel's Game" © 2010 by Jonathan Asche. "A Nose Commits Suicide" © 2010 by Daniel Allen Cox, reprinted with the author's permission from *Xtra* (May 2010). "Closet Case" © 2010 by Martin Delacroix. "The Last Picture. Show." © 2007, 2010 by James Earl Hardy. "The Boy in Summer" © 2009 by Shaun Levin, excerpted with the author's permission from *Snapshots of The Boy* (Treehouse Press, 2009). "Saving Tobias" © 2009 by Jeff Mann, reprinted with the author's permission from *Icarus 2* (Fall 2009). "Bodies in Motion" © 2010 by Johnny Murdoc. "And His Brother Came Too" © 2010 by Tony Pike. "Blossoms in Autumn" © 2005, 2009 by Boris Pintar; translation © 2009 by Rawley Grau, reprinted with the author's permission from *Family Parables* (Talisman House, 2009), originally published in Slovene as "*Cvetje v jeseni*" under the pseudonym Gojmir Polajnar in *Druzinske parabole* (Ljubljana: SKUC, 2005). "Counterrevolution" © 2010 by Thomas Rees. "Hump Day" © 2010 by Dominic Santi. "Barebacking" © 2010 by Simon Sheppard, reprinted with the author's permission from *Sodomy!* (Lethe Press). "I Sucked Off an Iraqi Sniper" © 2010 by Natty Soltesz, reprinted with the author's permission from the *BUTT* blog (June 2010). "Attackman" © 2010 by Rob Wolfsham.

For that fellow Asa
for (almost) twenty years of love
and for bringing us, for her last two years, Tiger-Lily

CONTENTS

FOREWORD

In the year since *Best Gay Erotica 2010* appeared, the market for written erotica has imploded.

Not for anthologies such as this one, thank goodness.

But the glory days of magazine erotica are gone.

In May 2009, the folks who owned Mavety Publications—founder George Mavety, enthusiastically heterosexual and much-married (with a reported dozen-plus children), died in 2000 while playing tennis in the hot sun—pulled the (butt) plug on a slew of gay glossies: *Torso, Honcho, Playguy, Inches, Latin Inches, Black Inches* and *Mandate.* The latter was the (grand)Daddy of the group; the first issue appeared in 1975, mere years after Stonewall, subtitled *Entertainment and Eros for Renaissance Men.*

The magazines weren't all naughty pics and one-handed prose, at least in the early days. A version of Larry Townsend's S/M bible, *The Leatherman's Handbook*, appeared in the first issue of *Torso*, and an edition of the book was available for years from Mavety's Modernismo Publications. Prophetically, the safe-sex plea "How to Have Sex in an Epidemic," by Michael Callen (1955-1993) and Richard Berkowitz, appeared in *Honcho*, expanded for publication as a book in 1983; the mags, in their best years (under editors Stan Leventhal, Jim Eigo and George T. Wallace) mixed the serious with the saucy, community-building with bulging jocks, culture with cock.

And though most men probably bought the magazines for the photos of muscled men and their generous members, the Mavety titles also nurtured the writing careers of dozens of queer writers—a majority of whom churned out formulaic fantasy fodder, but some of whom strove for a form of literary artistry.

The early years of this anthology—I started as series editor with the second edition, *Best Gay Erotica 1997*—drew heavily on work by the latter kind of writer, those who honed a talent for invoking arousal by penning porn at pennies a word for Mavety's mags, known around the office in those days (I was a friend of editor Leventhal and visited the editorial offices whenever I was in Manhattan) as the "sophisticates"—presumably to set them aside from the publisher's other magazines, among them *Juggs*, a title that leaves little to the imagination about the intended reader's fetish.

In recent years, I culled fewer stories from the gay glossies, as copycat publishers followed the Cleis lead and added porny anthologies to their catalogues. More outlets meant more writers, and the universe of erotic "bests" realized its own Big Bang evolution. So as a source for this series, the magazines won't be missed much. But as a training-wheels medium for up-and-cumming authors, their passing is to be lamented.

Richard Labonté
Bowen Island, British Columbia

INTRODUCTION: WHEN PORN IS EVERYWHERE, AND EVERYTHING IS PORN, WHAT IS THE PLACE FOR A BOOK LIKE THIS?

Now that I am capping my career by judging *Best Gay Erotica 2011,* I can tell you confidentially that I've never had such a cool gig. Hey, come on, what amazing luck! At first, a tad nervous, I asked some previous judges, what should I look for? To a man they advised, you don't have to worry about any looking, your gonads will tell you what you like. The stories will find you. What could be simpler?

I came of age in a different world. How different was it? It was so long ago that I wrote a pornographic book without having previously read one, and I acted in a porn film without having ever seen one. I didn't know what I was doing in either case, but thinking about it now, I suppose early on I conflated sex with representation or vice versa. It wasn't all about making marks. If you couldn't turn back to it and relive it, the sex one was having might as well not have happened. Even then I knew I was being a little bit less, well, spontaneous than most of my peers. More postmodern I guess, for I was all about the image as opposed to the reality. Well, the tide has caught up with me and how. I recently read a statistic that says that nearly every man who owns an iPhone (over 95 percent) has photographed his cock with it. While erect. That's a lot of photography, ain't it? (Not all of these hard cocks wind up on XTube—some are deleted immediately—some are lost among a staggering profusion of JPEGs. And then some disappear: do you know where your hard-on went? And still others, exiting sideways, fly the coop for now, only to return home later to haunt their owners.)

Theorist Jean Baudrillard complained, in one of his final essays, that the "illusion of desire" has been "lost in the ambient pornography." Thanks to the demolition of the taboo and the triumph of marketing, we have "moved into the transsexual." He didn't mean "transsexual" as you and I understand it, but as sexuality made literally, and relentlessly, transparent, visible. "In reality," he wrote (in "The Conspiracy of Art"), "there is no longer any pornography, since it is virtually everywhere. The essence of pornography permeates all visual and televisual techniques." I wondered what previous *BGE* judges had made of the reality Baudrillard cites here. When porn is everywhere, and everything is porn, what is the place for a book like this one? Last year Blair Mastbaum spoke to this directly, arguing that in the age of the Internet, it is precisely the book that removes the "transparency" from the erotic.

Words bring porn back into the private realm. Words put the erotic back in your mind. You conjure up the images when you're reading, with cues and hints from the author.

It's not as though Baudrillard was a Puritan, far from it; instead he was pointing out that you have to be clear-sighted enough to recognize that porn is being made available to us in the service of a market cynical enough to reward us with sexual pleasure in exchange for giving up our sense of "witness." Emanuel Xavier, who selected the stories for *BGE 2008*, made this point in the very first sentence of his introduction. When sex is everywhere around us, he wrote, then it's "easy to forget we are a nation at war." Sex mutates into the front pages of newspapers, all over the Internet, used to sell everything from cars to shoes to kitchen appliances. Gay sex is fashionable and mainstream. Even if it's subtle, all one has to do is pick up a magazine or turn on the television. I would be a hypocrite to claim not to indulge in such pleasures because I would rather focus on the realities of the world. Let's face it—if every consenting adult could enjoy sex without repercussions, the world would be a better place.

Well, until I read this I had never connected my addiction to porn to my utopian romanticism. So that's great. (One doesn't have to be a strict deconstructionist to intuit that the war in Iraq lurks behind all the stories in this book, no matter what they're ostensibly "about," just as the specter of AIDS haunted fiction in the '80s and early '90s. It's only that the war rarely appears as overtly and in such full strength as it does in the present volume, in the book's shortest story (a homoepathic dose?), Natty Soltesz's "I Sucked Off an Iraqi Sniper.")

James Lear's introduction to *BGE 2009* made it even easier, arguing that a sex story is essentially a conservative act. "It sets out to do a job: get the reader interested, get the reader aroused and get the reader off. If it doesn't do these three things, then, in my book, it isn't erotic fiction. It may be many other things, but if it's not primarily an inspiration to masturbation, it doesn't belong here."

A smorgasbord of great stories awaits your attention within the pages of *BGE 2011*. Before the brilliance of these authors, my own writing seems haphazard, incomplete. Can I make amends by spreading before you, like caviar on Ritz crackers, the best sex writers anywhere?

Dreams of all kinds, mostly erotic ("I dreamt of a doctor armed with latex gloves exploring my asshole") flit though Shane Allison's poetic and powerful "I Dreamt." Eric Karl Anderson's "Beauty #2" is a Warhol and Leigh Bowery–inspired saturnalia in which circuit boy flirts with fetish top at the annual Folsom Street Fair and at a downtown Manhattan hotel; revenge ensues. For those keeping track, revenge also moves the undead hero of Jeff Mann's uncanny "Saving Tobias," who targets a handsome, homophobic state senator on a drizzly February morning. Guys, you'll go for this one or my name's not Kevin Killian.

Have you ever desired a favorite video performer, an amateur perhaps, one to whom you return and return, desperate to plumb his mystery? If so, you'll relate to Thomas Rees's "Counterrevolution," with its boy jerking off in a claw-footed bathtub. James Earl Hardy's magnificent "The Last Picture. Show." is nearly a novel's worth of material in a single story, a generous and imaginative gift from a favorite author. Know what, I think some of these guys must have a direct hookup to my fantasies: the straight high school jock who returns humbly, eight years later, to the once-scorned gay boy and offers to romance him: thanks, Johnny Murdoc—I've just ruined another suit thanks to that one ("Bodies in Motion").

Like it or not, porn is always a blend between the everyday and the outré. Martin Delacroix, in "Closet Case," tells a familiar story of the married guy with a taste for dick, but then he brings in a surprise ending worthy of Rod Serling, which just makes the story hotter. Not to mention more plausible. Only a control freak would insist on absolute plausibility in porn, but I get a charge out of Boris Pintar's authentic Slovenian hustlers and johns, in "Blossoms in Autumn." Pintar knows whereof he speaks; you can practically smell the sex desperation flying off his middle-aged hero. Quaint as it seems, love powers the best of these stories, but it's not the kind of love your mother and father wanted for you; it's a love with ice in its mouth and fire in its ass.

Reading these stories will get you hot: that's their claim on you. Stroll with me down the incestuous Oxford streets of "And His Brother Came Too." (Tony Pike doesn't mince words when he titles his stories.) Unwind with me down at strip night at Chico, in the San Gabriel Valley on "Hump Day" (by Dominic Santi) and watch the sexiest dancer in California lose his pants in your palm. Voraciously gobbling down these stories, two or three at a time, I had to keep slowing myself down and remembering the wise words of Blair Mastbaum, James Lear, Emanuel Xavier. Xavier especially with his delightful image of the editor surrounded by empty Kleenex boxes, heaps of cumrags. You know what you want because it tells you where it will take you. Zero to a hundred in three or four paragraphs. As Lear said, "If a story can entertain or enlighten as well, that's great, but those included in this volume have one mission in mind—to help you, the reader, to a good orgasm."

This collection turns out to have no story by my favorite gay male sex writer, Thom Wolf of County Durham in England. Seems he didn't submit anything to this year's contest. Oh, well, this gives me the chance to dedicate my labors to him. Dear Thom, every time I got hard reading these stories, I turned my hard-on east in your direction. Every time I jerked off (or, as you would say, "emptied my balls"), I thought of you. Until I met you, I didn't really know what sex was, nor writing either. As for you, Richard Labonté, thanks for letting me into this (radical? conservative? totalizing? progressive?) world of yours; and now help me up, boys, I'm not as young as I used to be.

Kevin Killian

BEAUTY #2

Eric Karl Anderson

We go to the San Francisco Folsom Street Fair to laugh at the fags. Passing the gate guarded by drag queens with painted faces and wimples, we drop five-dollar bills into their charity buckets. "Go forth and sin more," the darling mustached freaks say to me. The streets are filled with them: overweight men in tight leather harnesses, an explosion of curly gray hair on their chests; anemic, topless skinheads in their twenties wearing bleached denim jeans; muscular, bearded doms wearing nothing but jock-straps and skin that is seared by huge blocks of faded tattoos, whose strut imitates fabled warriors. There are booths pushing fetish gear and an area with a spanking bench over which a handsome man bends wearing nothing but tube socks and cleats. In our Abercrombie & Fitch, with our stylishly cropped hair and clean-shaven jaws, we stand out from the crowd more than the straight tourists who have wandered into this kinky festival.

Our group traveled up to San Francisco from L.A. for a

weekend jaunt, a spontaneous fun trip organized at the last minute by our single friend Matt.

"I want to go to Folsom to hook up with a guy I met online," he told us. "And not just anyone. The director of the whole event. We've been exchanging such hot messages!"

We are fastidious about our grooming and the clothes we put on that morning before the event although we know we won't fit in at the fair, and we tell ourselves that we won't care what these people think anyway. Our group has unspoken rules. Underwear is important to us. Ginch Gonch are vulgar. Aussiebums are passé. Calvin Klein are incomparable. Our ornate occasional tables are decorated with bowls of artichokes. Our wallpaper is Leigh Bowery–inspired. Our Warhol lithographs have special meaning to us. Our floors are ebonized to give a glossy shine beneath our feet. The books on our shelves are decorative. We sit on uncomfortable sculptural Chinese chairs watching television-show box sets on our plasma screens. I myself don't come from money, but the others are good enough to overlook this due to the high-paying, intensely difficult job I have at Reuters and fight brutally to keep. We compete to make the best desserts, perfecting the art of baking Sacher Tortes, dacquoises and crumble-topped fruit muffins. But we never ever eat them. They are put on display and discarded after four days. Our diets are high protein, and we eat nothing after seven P.M. except what comes in cocktail glasses. We are all coupled, but we barely ever have sex with our partners. And when we do it's only cock to cock, never anything anal. Nothing messy. We jerk off in secret watching other men have sex in the steam rooms of gyms. We flirt with each other's partners via instant messenger. We rate the men on TV into categories of those who we'd "do" and "not do." Our heroines are women who inhale men and spit them out. Sex is embroidered into every thought of our daily lives, but we never do it. It's all intention, potential and expectation.

The only exception is Matt, the token single pet of our group, who entertains us with stories of his sexual conquests. Matt aspires to sleep with all the gay celebrities. He screwed a top presenter from E! Entertainment. He fumbled with Rufus Wainwright's limp dick when the singer was in a drugged haze. He made out with Rupert Everett. He fingered Jake Shears at a party. He shared a candlelit dinner with Neil Patrick Harris. He claims to have sucked off Anderson Cooper, but none of us believe him. And now he's determined to do the organizer of the world's largest fetish party as a cursory nod to the kinky fuck-heads of the gay community.

After entering the fair, we take time to marvel at the spectacles on show and laugh at these sincere physical expressions of the internal freak. Handsome young men walk on all fours pulled along by leashes held by arrogant, ugly, older men. Mean-looking punks walk along the street shirtless with pierced nipples and spiked colorful Mohawks. Men who are practically naked lumber through the crowd wearing spiked masks that entirely envelope their heads. Elaborately made-up drag queens wearing policewomen's uniforms give high-pitched screams. A black man wearing a white tuxedo drags behind him a chained white man wearing a black tuxedo. Women wearing tight latex pants bare their breasts with their nipples covered only by sparkling jeweled caps. Some men and women are decked out in elaborately detailed full Victorian garb. People either go to extreme lengths to pose or are entirely lost in looking, a bewitching, sexually exciting exchange.

It becomes evident fairly quickly that no one is noticing us with our clean-cut look. This annoys us. We walk impatiently among the crowd searching for Matt's online hookup, eyeing up the stalls flaunting their wares: Fetish gear. Disciplinary equipment. Dildos. Lubricant. A shirtless man in his late forties saunters past wearing a blood-flow-strangling-tight pair of leather pants, his voluminous stomach spilling over the studded waistband of it.

"Check out the muffin top," Sylvan says.

"Not so much muffin top as stuffed crust," is Jay's retort. We all giggle while the fat man barrels past.

"Sergei!" Matt calls to a bald, muscular, bearded man in the distance. He is holding a clipboard and talking frantically to two guys in leather kilts. Matt strolls up to him. The rest of us follow cautiously behind. Sergei points to a map of the streets and says to the men, "Just make sure this area is kept clear for the next act." The kilted men leave and Sergei looks at Matt's face, showing only a couple of brief seconds of uncertainty before his face lights up in recognition. "Matey77 isn't it? Hey, buddy, how's it going?"

"Cool!" Matt chirps excitedly. He sucks in his already concave stomach.

"So you made it. That's great." He tucks his arm around Matt's waist in a familiar way and takes a long drink from a plastic cup filled with beer.

Sergei has a wide inviting smile, clean-shaven head, short facial hair, dark bold eyebrows and bright blue eyes. He wears a tight, solidly black uniform shirt that strains against his broad chest and muscular arms. A hint of what looks like a dark blue comet tattooed on his left arm creeps out from under the sleeve. His stern face is filled with compassion. It's obvious that numerous lovers would eagerly bare themselves for this god of the heavens and earth.

"Yeah, we've been looking around," Matt laughs derisively, scanning the scene around us. "This is...quite the crowd."

"Yes. Have a blast, you guys," he nods to us before Matt can do introductions. "I'll catch up with you later." He pats Matt on the back and rushes off to speak to a DJ.

Sergei glances at me while he goes past and hands me his cup of beer. I know in an instant that he can give me what I need. Watching him walk away, the guys turn to Matt with faces contorted in quizzical humor as if to say, *This is what we came all the way here for?* Clearly the masculine busy man doesn't meet our standards. Matt says, "Let's have a look around. I'll see if I can get a minute alone with him." I sip from the cup, savoring the wet half-moon ring on the cup's rim where Sergei's lips have been.

Matt wants to linger, hoping to catch another moment with the healthy, energetic event organizer and seduce him. Our group stations itself beside one of the drinks tents, sipping mojitos while scanning the crowd and making catty comments. We are like explorers lost in a foreign land. I try to take Sylvan's hand and put it around my waist to protect me, but he's too busy checking the news headlines on his BlackBerry. Looking at the crowd it's difficult to distinguish the meeting between two old friends who vigorously embrace and squeeze each other's butts from that of two new friends who spontaneously give rough kisses and quick, hungry gropes. At one point we spy Sergei in the distance smiling amid a jostling group of excited leathermen. He is holding a flogger aloft like a thunderbolt. Matt tries to make his way through the crowd to him. But, by the time he arrives at the group, Sergei is nowhere to be seen. The air is humming with possibility. There are strict rules and no rules at the same time. The vulgar and obscene are admired as beautiful by the majority of the crowd, whereas we find it laughable and sad. Soon we pick up on common signs, especially among the older leathermen. We see men with sunken cheeks and sickly

looking emaciated bodies that signal that they have consumed
spoiled fruit and might soon pay for it with their lives.

"This isn't funny anymore," Jay says emphatically. "I've had
enough of this fucking AIDS death camp."

Signs of death offend us. We return to L.A.

Weeks pass. During this time my erotic imagination begins to
filter the atmosphere that I had witnessed at the fair into an
entirely new sensibility. I begin to see through Sergei's clear blue
eyes. Mysterious elements within me erupt to the surface. Staying
late at work to compile a report analyzing statistics on global
precious metals, I find myself conducting an extensive and frantic
Internet search on this man I'd only glimpsed briefly. I study
the fetish fair's website, fan sites and social networking sites,
tracking down information and pictures of Sergei. Every detail I
collect adds to my craving for him: he is of Russian heritage; he
took a vacation to Australia; he's had a boyfriend for six years;
he is a fan of British sitcoms; he's worked at Folsom for three
years helping to raise thousands and thousands of dollars for
charities while throwing a massive fetish party out in the open;
in early photos he has small simple tattoos on his arms. but these
have recently developed into full blocks of intricately designed
patterns and color. Finding a public conversation between Sergei
and a friend of his on one social networking website, I discover a
casual comment he made about a kinky dating website. I quickly
join this website and scan the profiles of San Francisco members.
Finally I find his profile. By now it is three in the morning in
our starch-white open-plan office, but I still spend another hour
drinking the gold mine of information contained in his pictures,
personal description and lists of fetishes. He prefers being a top;
he likes it sweaty; he is HIV positive: each revelatory fact makes
him more perfect in my feverish imagination.

Sergei invades my daytime thoughts and my nighttime self quickly smothers my efficient lively everyday persona. The small motions of daily life are infused with a perverse devotion for this virtual stranger I've inexplicably become obsessed with. I jostle through papers on my desk without noticing their contents. I stand beside the water cooler with my coworkers listening to complaints about the new intern who can't spell and laugh with disinterest. I sit at a table in a fashionable new Asian-American restaurant with my friends sipping warmed sake and discuss the dishiest waiters. All the while, I think about how to alter my appearance, modify myself to become more desirable to him. My mind is polluted by passion. Suddenly, I declare to my friends that I want to grow a beard and get some leather pants. Their eyes are filled with disgust, and Sylvan's arched eyebrow lets me know how disposable I am.

Later on, fresh out of the shower, I practice posing in the mirror inhabiting a tough-guy persona and snap photos of myself. I spend some time creating a gallery of sexually suggestive pictures and upload it to my profile on the kinky website. Then I laboriously compose a profile description that I think will cater to Sergei's tastes: *New masculine sub hungry to explore: very obedient, very fit, very frisky.*

It's some indeterminable time in the night. I send Sergei a quick flirtatious email through the dating website's messaging system. Then I jerk my hard cock while imagining Sergei's boot stepping on the small of my naked back, lifting my head with an iron-gripped fistful of hair and hearing the muscular god whispering what a dirty cunt I am. I want to crawl along the grimy floor struggling to kiss his toes, bare my ass to him for a whipping, sleep chained to the foot of his bed waiting for the tiniest sign of affection. I crave the feel of his hand around my throat while he forces his lips upon mine and then wrenches open my mouth to swallow his thick dick so far that I gag, a punch to the gut and his knee in my balls. I want him to beat me, leaving me gasping for breath and begging to sniff his sweaty armpits. He'll clean me by pissing on my naked form in a ghetto's concrete alleyway, then force my face into his ass to lick his hole out, and he'll fuck my cold trembling body and leave me covered in grime for passersby to spit at. Enslaved, I'll run my tongue along the dirty underside of his toilet seat, offer him all my money and possessions and suck his dick clean after he's fucked his boyfriend. He'll screw my faggot ass at a second's notice, pounding me with such force that my bent naked body will snap in two and my face will be rubbed raw against the floor. I will abstain and deny myself all comforts so that any sensations of pleasure or pain I feel will be because he deemed it.... Sylvan is sleeping peacefully in our four-poster Queen Anne mahogany bed under ivory silk sheets. The streetlamps cast an amber glow that penetrates our blinds. Sticky semen oozes between the fingers of my clenched fist, and my body smarts from innumerable imaginary bruises. It's almost time for me to get up for work.

Sylvan and I sit at our antique Shaker dining room table in the morning eating carefully measured portions of steaming oatmeal with thin slivers of banana out of Jasper Conran Wedgwood bowls. Our laptops are open and we are spending this half hour together over breakfast checking email, blogs and news websites.

"Jay's friend Michael is DJ-ing at Club Ripples. I told Tony and Sam I'd meet them there for shots at eight."

"Fab. I've got after-work drinks for Sahara at Fubar, but I can catch a cab there by nine."

"Tony's sis Jessica might be there too."

"Ugh! Have you seen her latest Facebook picture? Jess should really slow down on the Botox before she has a total bat face. But maybe she should go back under the knife and do something about that nose."

"Seriously. I mean, hello! That nose hasn't been in fashion since the late nineties."

"Doubt it would help that horse face of hers. Or her hyena laugh."

"I know. And she laughs at the stupidest shit. Things that aren't even funny."

"She's got the personality of a jellyfish. She's a total coke head too."

"She's got a killer body though. Great knockers."

"Fantastic breasts."

"We should get her over for dinner."

"Yeah, and her sexy boyfriend Drake."

We down our cappuccinos and kiss before leaving for work.

Sergei and I exchange several messages over the next week. I don't mention seeing him at the fair or that I've been tracking him over cyberspace. I pretend to have stumbled across his profile when searching for a hookup. His messages are clipped erotic half sentences that sear my imagination. We chat tentatively about meeting up, but I don't want to see him anywhere near my life here. I want to give myself to him on some foreign ground, where the echoes of my screams as he devours me can't be heard by anyone familiar. I read another discussion between him and a friend on a social networking site, discovering that he'll be at a leather fair in New York City in three weeks.

The next morning I tell Sylvan that I have to attend a conference for work in New York City.

* * *

I enter Sergei's suite at a fashionable downtown hotel. The paint looks fresh on the walls, the air feels carefully circulated and there are sleek modern lines to the decor. Black-and-white framed photographs featuring dramatically lit monuments and statues adorn the walls. He shutters the large window view of placid, gray sky and bulky, concrete buildings by pressing a button. I say that I need to have a piss, at which he nods and says he'll pour us a drink. The black marble stone bathroom has a glass counter and silver washbasin. Numerous small orange bottles filled with pills are carefully lined up on one side. I look at these in wonder and excitement, studying and instantly forgetting the many prescription drug names like a tourist. I hear the thumping introductory beats of some music through the half-closed door. He is waiting, the man I am trembling with need to give myself to. I flush the toilet and quickly turn on and off the tap, making a show to hide the fact that I just wanted a moment alone to savor the anticipation.

The room's lights have been substantially dimmed. His iPod is set on a stylish stereo dock that is glowing blue. A thumping electronic beat rings out through the speakers, and a mournful Central European–sounding female voice begins singing a low-pitched melody. He walks up to me and tilts his head to the side as if sizing me up. I'm frozen in place as he grabs my jaw and forces his mouth onto mine. His kiss is wet and deep and urgent. As he opens his mouth to enclose mine, his body begins to grind against me. I respond and fit myself against him, treasuring the feel of his muscular arm as it encloses me and the gruff scrape of his beard against my smooth face. I'm only aware of the music in my ears and of his touch. He releases me and walks away so quickly I almost fall forward. He changes the song to one with quick drumbeats and an electronic hum. Two women sing mournfully over each other. He slides out of his clothes, letting them fall to the floor, and steps up to me again, fully naked with his hard cock bobbing up and down. This is a man of such strength, confidence and lusty beauty that I'm completely entranced. I kiss him again and let him undress me, only helping to undo my complex belt buckle when he fumbles with it. I'm ready to be struck down. Fully naked we rub against each other for some time until he wrestles me onto the floor. His rough face slides down my body, digging at the dark alcoves of it with his tongue and gripping my limbs in his strong hands. He directs me onto my front and laps at my ass. In my mind, I whisper for him to fuck me and then I'm shouting it aloud, my voice in combat with the thumping music. He stands and retrieves a condom from the pocket of his crumpled jeans on the carpet.

Painfully I twist my neck around to look up at him. I slam my fists against the floor with my ass still angled up in air. "Fuck me bareback! I want to feel your cock inside me!"

Sergei stares at me with the metallic square wrapper in his hand and his hard cock pointing upward. I shout it again. I beg him to fuck me and shove his skin into my hole.

"I told you in a message I'm HIV positive. It's in my profile: only safe sex."

I stand and wrap my arms around him hungrily, kissing and groping him. He responds and rubs against me. I take the condom from his hand and throw it to the floor, then pull him on top of me on the bed and lift my legs so they are over his shoulders.

"Fuck me," I demand.

I look up at him angrily. His eyebrows narrow and he sneers at me in fury. He throws my legs off, stands up and firmly says no. He begins to dress and I begin to cry, first slowly and then with strong heaving sobs. I curl up on top of the crisp bedspread and hug my knees to my chest. I feel him crawl behind me, enclosing me warmly in his arms, kissing my burning ears and telling me it's going to be all right. We fall asleep in a strange sort of embrace.

In the morning I stare at his sleeping naked form. His hideously large skull covered in a thin layer of taut near-transparent skin reveals purple-blue veins. His tattoos look slightly faded, and it's easy to imagine how sickly they will appear once his skin starts to sag and wrinkle. Patches of his skin are blotched red from sleeping on his arm. His mouth hangs slightly open and emits a choking hiss of a snore. Numerous lines have permanently creased the sides of his eyes and his forehead. Small pink pimples dot his shoulders from where he's plucked or shaved the hair. Lube mixed with my anal juices left faint brown stains on his fingers. He is old and ugly and dying. I am disgusted by the sight of him. I want to punish him.

I slip quietly into the marble bathroom. The hard floor freezes my sensitive naked feet. I pick up and examine the numerous small orange medicine bottles. My mirror image appears young, painfully thin, and my skin has a healthy glow under the recessed lighting. The pills make a satisfying clicking sound as I turn them in my hands, studying the complex names printed on the labels. I open them and pour the contents of each one into my hands until I have a large palm full of variously shaped white, cream, yellow and blue pills. These I tip into the toilet bowl. I carefully recap each medicine bottle and put it back in its place on the countertop. Then I have a long piss and flush the toilet. There are some splashes of water on the taps and the glass surface, which I wipe down until they shine, and I'm careful to leave the towels neatly straightened on their racks. I dress and leave before Sergei wakes up.

* * *

On the flight back to the West Coast I stare into my glass of champagne, watching the bubbles scream to the surface. The sound is barely audible against the electronic screech of the aircraft sailing through the sky and the boisterous businessmen in the seats nearby who sling back glasses of scotch and tear carnivorously into the prettily arranged beef empanada. I refuse all of the courses offered by the immaculately presented stewardess, and I choose instead to only pick through a fruit salad and make friends with the bottles on the alcohol trolley.

Sinking back into the plush leather seat, I glance out the small oval window at the blue slate of sky hiding the surface of Middle America. It's a comfort that we're traversing the length of the country without even noticing the numerous banal towns and tedious cities scattered over the rural landscape. I imagine that this plane is a sort of escape pod that has delivered me from the little town where I was born. It still exists down there somewhere, inhabited by my family and childhood friends, who writhe miserably in their provincial lives and are smothered by tedium. My heart actually races when I think how I've escaped what could have been my life. I'm balanced upon the edge of a cliff watching a lava flow engulf a village and its hundreds of screaming inhabitants. I'm in a life raft floating on a treacherous ocean watching a ship in flames collapsing into the roaring water. I've wrestled a tornado that's destroyed everything, and now I'm returning to my enchanted city. This is the only way I know how to survive.

I can't afford this first-class flight, but I booked it on my credit card anyway. I'm nearing the limits on several cards and have no idea how I'll pay them off, despite the good salary and generous bonuses I receive. I suspect Sylvan is in similar financial trouble, but we never discuss money. No one in our group cares about money; we simply expect it to be there. I've worn my new Gucci shirt to meet Sylvan at the airport—although he wasn't certain if he'd have time to make it out to LAX, and I might just see him back at the apartment. That is, unless he got caught up having drinks with colleagues. In which case, I might not see him until the next morning.

ATTACKMAN

Rob Wolfsham

Alex liked it when Max Weston treated him like shit. The star attackman of the lacrosse team shoved the skinny skater to the ground and straddled his back, squeezing Alex's sides with his knees as the younger boy writhed beneath him. Max pressed Alex's skateboard against the back of his head, pushing his face into damp, cold weeds. Sweaty jocks laughed. One lacrosse player said, "Max, c'mon, get off him, man."

Max tossed the skateboard aside and released the shaggy-haired skater, unfolding into a long-boned nineteen-year-old boy.

Alex rolled onto his back, grabbed his skateboard and swung it like a bat at Max.

Guys made stupid *ooh* sounds.

Max jumped back grinning, flashing the gap between his two front teeth. "Faggot wants to get tough, huh?" Freckles dotted his high cheekbones. His chestnut hair was buzzed on the sides, slicked forward on top and spiked up at his forehead. He snarled through his piggish nose. He looked like an all-American teen from a fifties advertisement for baseball or killing Russians.

Alex stood up. Weed stems and grass leaves flaked from his baggy clothes. He rubbed his nest of dyed black hair, threaded with grass. More grass clung to his pearly face and sharp nose. He held his skateboard like a sword. "Go get syphilis again."

Max cupped his hands around his mouth, walking backward toward his friends, swaggering. "Faggot, next time you get near my car, I'm going to shove your face in more than just grass."

Guys laughed. Alex kept the lip of his skateboard aimed at the receding pack of jocks.

Mr. Albrecht, the only cool English teacher at the school, marched up to Max Weston and his gang. "Guys, guys, touching boys means detention. Don't let me fuck up your season."

Max spat into the grass, barely missing Mr. Albrecht's khaki pants. The athlete and his crowd walked past the short, red-faced teacher, who had thinning hair and big square glasses.

Mr. Albrecht approached Alex, still in his defense posture. "Shields down?" the teacher asked, curling a smile.

Alex let his skateboard fall to the ground. "What did you say?"

"Enough, I hope."

"Fucking diplomacy," Alex said. He tossed his board on the sidewalk and skated off through the parking lot, weaving through dozens of cars lined around campus waiting to pick up students. It was February of senior year. He had just turned eighteen with only three months left until the freedom of graduation, the freedom of complete uncertainty. Alex skateboarded down the sidewalk along a busy boulevard under a heatless sun, wheels clicking over segments of concrete.

He tightened the blue hoodie around his face and plucked

smaller stems of weeds off his clothes. Cars zoomed down the road. Max Weston's black Chevy Tahoe roared by. Nothing happened. Alex felt empty.

The skater reached home and entered through the back gate and back door, shuffling through the laundry room past a rumbling washer and dryer.

Alex's mother stood in the kitchen holding up a big sheet of lasagna pasta. "Italian night," she sang happily as Alex walked by.

"Oh," he said. He burst into his room, locked the door, stripped naked, flopped onto his bed and fingered his cock. He pushed his fingers into new bruises on his legs and sides. He imagined his ankles suspended in the air, skin raw from rope burn. He imagined things Max Weston's body could do. He gazed at his ceiling photo collage of skaters and snowboarders printed from random blogs and cut out. His eyelids fell and his feet spread. He jacked himself slowly.

In the wet grass of an endless field, Max Weston stood glistening and sun-licked, naked except for black padded lacrosse gloves with bumpy grips. Alex was on all fours, his pale, hairless asscheeks facing Max. Fog encased them like hot steam. He was filthy, covered in grass stains and dirt.

The lacrosse team lounged nude on bleachers, their scratched knees stretched apart, cocks out, casual observers of ritual.

Max's gloved fists gripped a lacrosse stick. The plastic of the gloves crinkled, tightening over his knuckles before the lacrosse star growled and swung the stick across Alex's back. Netting popped against the skater's bony spine and shoulder blades. Alex groaned, throwing his head back, mouth agape. A waffle pattern glowed red on his back.

The lacrosse attackman got on his knees and shoved the head of the stick between Alex's legs, scooping up Alex's dangling balls and cock in the netted cup, encasing them. He jerked the stick up, nearly lifting Alex off the ground. The skater cried out in a mix of pain and ecstasy, balls straining against the netting.

Max's glove grabbed the skater's neck and yanked him against his sinewy long chest. "I want you to enjoy this," he breathed into Alex's ear. He rammed himself into Alex with no preparation or warning. Alex cried out but three fingers clawed into his mouth, then four, gagging him. The lacrosse player fucked him, chewed his ear with his gapped teeth, pulled on the inside of his cheek, called him shit eater as his flexing quads slapped the skater's asscheeks. Alex came.

A loud knock on his door jolted Alex from his daydream. "Don't come in," he said, panting, sucked back to a reality where he lay on his back, hair in his red face, scooping cum off his chest. "I'm about to shower."

His mother spoke through the door: "I was just going to say, I got an email from your English teacher today? We're going to talk about that later, okay?"

"Leave me alone, thank you," Alex said. He lay in silence watching the door. He exhaled and dangled his fingers over his face, drooling the snotty webs of cum into his mouth.

Nothing happened for a week. Mr. Albrecht's threat seemed to keep Max and the jocks away from Alex, until the day when the general P.E. class shared the locker room with the lacrosse team. Alex changed alone in his corner several rows of lockers away from everyone else. The rest of the guys crowded on the other side, changing and chatting.

Mr. Albrecht entered the musty concrete room wearing blue bike shorts, an orange tank top, sweatbands around his forehead and wrists and a whistle dangling from his neck. As the

English and drama teacher, he made his physical education duties a performance piece.

"Mr. Albrecht," said one student as the teacher passed. "I'm sharing a locker with Jason, and he's not back yet. Can you open it?"

"Guys, this is ridiculous," Mr. Albrecht said. "There are enough lockers. Look over there." He pointed to the other side of the room where Alex was pulling his shirt off, revealing a brilliantly pale, skinny body.

"That section is closed due to AIDS," Max said. His lacrosse buddies laughed.

"What?" Mr. Albrecht asked with genuine confusion.

"Nothing," Max said pulling his shirt off over his head and tossing it into a locker.

"No," Mr. Albrecht said. "I'm serious. What did you mean by that?"

Jimmy, a Mexican jock with a thick accent, said with confused concern, "No one wants a homo to look at them."

Mr. Albrecht looked over at Alex, sitting shirtless, untying bright purple shoelaces on his Vans.

Mr. Albrecht said, "If I hear anyone say that word again they're getting an in-school suspension."

No one said anything.

The teacher pointed his clipboard at everyone. "Take your shit out of the lockers. You're all spreading out over there. Assigned lockers from now on."

The guys groaned and shuffled. Even Alex looked up and said, "Fuck no." Most of the lacrosse team didn't budge.

"I'm serious," Mr. Albrecht said. He poked his thick square glasses up his nose.

"You can't make us go over there," Max said.

The English teacher looked at his clipboard. "Actually I can.

When the lacrosse team is in here during my P.E. period, you follow my rules. You can ask Coach Starkey."

All the guys started shuffling unenthusiastically, spreading through the locker room with their books and clothes, slamming doors. Max was the only one who didn't move.

Mr. Albrecht said, "I'll let Coach Starkey know your undying crush on Alex Ritter is preventing you from functioning normally in here."

"What?" Max laughed. He grew bright red and muttered, "Fucking pervert."

Others who heard stopped what they were doing and watched.

"You just got in-school suspension," Mr. Albrecht said.

"I didn't say anything."

The teacher started writing on his clipboard. "That'll cut into practice time, too."

"No, c'mon," Max said. He quickly took his stuff over to Alex and dropped it next to him. Alex stepped away. Max threw his arms around the bony, shaggy-haired skater, squeezing him. "Look, we're buddies. He likes it."

Alex slinked out from under Max's grip. The athlete yanked the skater back against his chest and wrapped his arms around his stomach, lightly tickling him.

Alex squirmed. "Get off me."

Max grinned at Mr. Albrecht from over Alex's bony shoulder.

"Faggots," Jimmy laughed.

Mr. Albrecht headed for the locker room door. "I don't have time for this. You're seniors. Act like it. Get changed and get out of here."

When the door shut, Max shoved Alex against a locker. "You're gonna fucking get me suspended."

"I didn't do anything," Alex said.

"Yeah, except be a faggot."

The bell rang and everyone had finished changing except Alex and Max. The rest of the lacrosse team and general P.E. class shuffled out of the room, leaving the skater and athlete alone.

"Now I'm going to be late," Max said.

"You care about class?" Alex asked. They sat down several feet away from each other.

"Fuck you, homo," Max said.

"No. I'm trying to stay STD free."

"Can you shut the fuck up? I'm clean now, okay? Becky Benson is the whore. It wasn't my fault."

They said nothing for a while. The lacrosse player pulled his shorts off, quickly wrapped a towel around himself and stood.

"What are you doing?" Alex asked.

"What does it look like? I'm showering."

"We have like four minutes until class."

"You're not going to shower?"

"General P.E. doesn't have to shower."

"That's fucking gross, man," Max said. "You were just running around outside for an hour. Fucking shower."

"No, I don't want to shower," Alex said.

"Take your fucking shorts off and shower, faggot," Max said.

Alex stared ahead at the blue caged doors of the row of lockers, hiding a creeping thrill in his lips and loins. "Fuck off. I don't have a towel."

Max pulled an extra towel from his locker and threw it at Alex. It hit him in the side of the head and fell to the floor. Max walked to the showers, big feet slapping his flip-flops. Alex yanked his shorts off, wrapped the towel around himself and followed.

They showered in silence for sixty seconds in the open tile

room, five nozzles away from each other, rapidly scrubbing themselves. Alex looked at Max Weston once or twice by accident, taking in the solid glutes of the lacrosse player's ass. A river delta of Old Spice soap suds seeped down Max's pale cheeks and quads and long powerful calf muscles. A thick cut cock dangled under a soapy bush.

Max side-eyed Alex's glistening, bony frame. Alex's shaggy black hair tickled his shoulders and thick strands hung over his deep-set eyes and sharp nose. Their eyes caught each other but moved on as though enjoying the scenery of some imaginary landscape behind their bodies. But Alex glimpsed a semi-boner out of the corner of his eye.

They dried, dressed and walked out separate doors of the locker room as the late bell rang.

"Where were you?" Alex's friend Greg asked when the skater took his seat in the back of a noisy, aimless history class. The teacher flipped through channels on a TV attached to the ceiling.

Greg was a skinny nerd with thick, round glasses and brown, spiked hair. He liked to pretend to be stoned all the time. "I heard you got in a fight with Max Weston after P.E."

"It wasn't a fight," Alex said.

"I heard he shoved you."

"It wasn't a fight."

"Man, you gotta fight back and shit," Greg said, knuckling Alex's arm. "Gay power and shit, right?"

"I'm not going to fight Max Weston. Fuck coming out. I take it back. I should have waited until graduation."

"Dude, no one cares except Max Weston and his dumb jock friends. Look around the fucking room." Greg held his hand out to the noisy classroom packed with students talking and messing with their cell phones, some sitting on the floor. A young teacher in his midtwenties was putting a DVD in the TV. "This school has like three thousand people who don't care about anything, or would make fun of you for something else anyway. I'm not gay and I get called faggot all the time."

"Yeah, I know, but it's like he's obsessed with me."

"Okay, yeah, some people did think it was weird the other day when he, like, rode your ass on the ground and shoved your face in the grass."

"You saw that?"

"Yeah, the whole school saw it. Someone said you had a boner."

"I did not have a boner."

"Everyone saw your boner."

"Shut up," Alex said.

"Mr. Albrecht had a boner, too."

"Mr. Albrecht did jack shit," Alex said.

"I know. He's kind of lame, right? I heard he has kiddie porn. We should hack his laptop and try to find it."

"That's fucking retarded. You're not a hacker."

"Dude, did you shower?"

"No, leave me alone, man."

"Smells nice."

In newspaper club the next week, Alex worked on a news story about how Sarah Palin is the goddamn devil. Mr. Albrecht, the school newspaper coordinator, handed a letter to Monica, a giggly Vietnamese-American girl who was the chief editor.

"Alex, you'll want to see this." Mr. Albrecht said. "This was just sent to the newspaper email."

"We get emails?" Monica asked as she read the letter. Alex came over to look. It was a letter to the editor from Max Weston, a rant about the Gay-Straight Alliance club the school had started recently. In the letter the lacrosse player complained about how a Gay-Straight Alliance degraded the school and was a distraction to the learning environment. Every other word was misspelled.

"Wow, this is dumb," Monica said. "He can't talk about the learning environment when he's like functionally illiterate."

"Look at this part," Alex pointed halfway down the letter. "He asks why can't we have an Aryan Nations club since we have a GSA now. Holy shit."

"This letter makes him look really bad," Monica said. "He sounds like a Nazi."

"He is a Nazi," Alex said. "Monica, you have to write a response and run this letter with it."

"Now wait," Mr. Albrecht said. "We can't do that. That's a conflict of interest."

"What? How?" Alex said, his excitement draining.

"Monica is secretary of the Gay-Straight Alliance, and editor of this paper. She can't criticize someone for their opinion on the GSA if she's a member of the GSA."

"That's bullshit," Alex said.

"Alex."

"Monica is secretary of every club in school," Alex said. "She's not even gay."

The girl shrugged. "He is right. I just like being secretary."

They ran the letter at the end of the month, but with no editorial response. They let the lacrosse player's letter speak for itself.

The wheels of Alex's skateboard clicked over slabs of concrete on the sidewalk under a heatless sun. Cars zoomed down the adjacent road. A black Chevy Tahoe roared by. The tires screeched, rubber burning into pavement. The hulking vehicle seized to a stop ahead of Alex.

Alex pulled his hoodie tight around his face and slowed his skateboard, unsure what to do. The Tahoe's white reverse lights flashed, and the SUV screeched backward until it stopped next to Alex. Max Weston leaped out of the driver's seat into the busy road and marched around the front of the SUV. He shoved Alex right off his skateboard. Cars drove around the Tahoe, honking.

"What the fuck are you doing!" Alex shouted, jumping up from the grass.

The lacrosse star picked up the skateboard and threw it at Alex. It hit him in the chest and knocked him off balance. Max shoved Alex as he wobbled. The gangly skater tumbled down an embankment into a heavily wooded ditch.

"Think you're such a smart faggot?" Max marched down to Alex and kicked him with all his strength.

Alex rolled into a muddy patch and wheezed for air, clutching his stomach. The ditch blocked the view from the road.

Max grabbed the skater's hair and dragged him through the mud, then kicked again. "They want to fucking expel me!" the athlete shouted at the curled-up boy.

Alex panted and held his muddy palms up toward Max. Wind roared through the trees. "You wrote the email," Alex coughed.

"They say it's fucking hate speech! I'm gonna lose my lacrosse scholarship!" Max got on his knees, sinking into the mud. He slammed his fist into Alex's face.

Alex cried out and tried to roll away.

Max straddled him, squeezing his knees against the skater's ribs. "Tell them I didn't write it!"

"Fuck you!" Alex groaned, twisting. Blood trickled from a nostril. His hands were pinned under Max's knees. His face burned and throbbed.

"Fucking hell, man!" Max yelled, looking up at the dense swaying treetops, then down at Alex's bloodied red face.

The lacrosse star had been crying. Two dried trails ran from his eyes to his thin lips. The two trails terrified Alex more than his fists.

"Why do you have to be such a faggot?" Max grabbed Alex's chest, bunching up the skater's muddy hoodie in his fists like he wanted to rip something out.

"Get off of me," Alex breathed.

"Why do you like dick?"

"Get the fuck off of me!"

"Why are you a faggot!" Max yelled in his face like a machine on repeat.

"Fuck you!"

"What? You like this, right?" The athlete grabbed the skater's knees, spread them and slammed his crotch against his, athletic shorts grinding into baggy jeans.

"I don't!" The skater's eyes widened. He felt Max's solid boner poking his balls.

Max laughed. "Yeah, feel that? Like that?"

Alex moaned, unable to stop himself. He squirmed against Max's massive dick, blood rushing to his own.

"I got something now," Max grinned devilishly, flashing the gap between his front teeth. He grabbed Alex's crotch and pumped the skater's cock and balls through his jeans. "Look at you go, faggot."

"Fucking shit," Alex moaned, throwing his head back into the mud. The trail of blood from his nostril reached his lip. The orange sky peeked through the treetops. Mud matted his hair.

"Oh, yeah." Max's hand pumped Alex's growing boner, the violent friction hurting and teasing.

"Fuck," Alex moaned.

"Tell me you like it," Max said through his gritted teeth.

"Yeah," Alex breathed.

"You think of this shit when you jack off?"

Max pumped Alex harder, pounding his crotch with rage.

Alex nodded feverishly and grabbed the glimmering blue tent of Max's athletic shorts, easily pumping the loose hard cock.

"Oh, god," Max quivered. "Fucking good." The hairs on his arms and legs stood on end. The skater pumped with equal vigor. Max stopped pounding Alex's dick and fumbled with the buckle of the boy's wide cloth belt, pulling it apart and unzipping the skater's jeans.

Alex pulled Max's athletic shorts down trembling thighs, and his eight-inch cut cock flopped out. Peach-sized nuts dangled halfway to the ground. Max yanked the skater's baggy jeans down with his boxers, their dicks both exposed to the cool air. Max pressed his thickness against Alex's smaller dick and pumped them together in his fist.

Max's sweaty balls bounced on Alex's nuts. They moaned and Alex's asscheeks sank into the mud. The lacrosse player whimpered as he pumped their cocks furiously, a sound Alex never expected to hear from the athlete. The skater humped into Max's pumping hand, pushing into the warm space with Max's cock sliding against his. Everything got slick with precum. They were in bliss, oblivious to anything but the sex, pain and anger peeling away.

Mr. Albrecht's beat up Toyota pulled to a stop behind the black Chevy Tahoe on the side of the road. He turned on his emergency lights, got out and inspected the SUV. Traffic was light. An orange evening sun cast shadows. He went back to his car, but as he reached his door, he heard a groan of pain through the wind. He walked back to the Tahoe and looked down the embankment.

In the shadows of the densely packed trees at the base of the ditch, Max Weston was fucking Alex in the mud, doggy-style, fast, angry and silent. They had their clothes on, except that Alex's jeans and Max's athletic shorts were pulled down to their knees. Max cupped the skater's mud-smeared neck as he pounded his white, bony ass.

Mr. Albrecht stared in a trance, then got on his hands and knees, obscuring himself behind the embankment, but not enough to block his view.

He watched until they finished, holding his breath. They made no noise. The lacrosse player fell against the skater's body, pushing him down into the mud. They lay together, muddy, sweaty and spent. Alex's face appeared bloodied, but he was smiling. The athlete rested his lips on the skater's cheek. He pulled the skater's hair to turn his face so their lips touched and melted together. They tongued into each other, the athlete clutching the skater's hair.

The English teacher crawled away and went back to his car and drove home. He washed his face in hot water and stared in the bathroom mirror before scrubbing grass stains out of the knees of his khaki pants.

The next day when Alex told him he was the one who wrote the hate letter from Max Weston, the English teacher didn't know what to say except, "Okay."

"You're not going to ask me why?" Alex asked.

Mr. Albrecht looked somewhere else. "That's fine, Alex. I'll tell Principal Edwards."

"I already told her."

"That's good. Thank you, Alex."

The skater glanced at the English teacher's distant gaze before going back to his seat.

"What was that all about?" Monica asked. "You wrote the letter?"

"Yeah."

"Why? Do you *like* getting bullied or something?"

"Forget it. I just wanted to get him in trouble. I'm sorry."

"Oh, I don't care," Monica said. "It does make us look kind of bad, but I don't think anyone really reads anymore. It's weird Mr. Albrecht isn't more pissed."

"Yeah. He's probably just disappointed in me or something."

"He keeps staring at you. It's sort of creepy."

"Great. That means he's pissed."

The bell rang. In the densely packed hallway between classes, a foot tripped Alex. The skater toppled forward onto his hands and knees, backpack sliding away. The crowded hallway parted to make room. A male voice barked, "Watch it, faggot."

Alex stared at the faux-marble floor inches from his face, then looked up at the lacrosse attackman. Max Weston stood tall, fully dressed in padded gear, lacrosse stick planted on the tiled floor like a warrior. Just visible through the zoetrope of faces and bodies rushing through the hallway, a smirk crept onto Max's lips, which Alex matched with his own. Mr. Albrecht saw it all from his classroom doorway.

COUNTERREVOLUTION

Thomas Rees

It starts and he's sitting in this claw-foot tub. I can tell it's a claw-foot by the way it's set off from the wall behind it by a shadow. It makes me miss the tub from my youth, off-white like coffee creamer. But I never masturbated in that tub.

He looks too young, but that's probably because he's shaved like most of the younger things nowadays. Why is that? A generation that grew up on Internet pornography will obviously have different standards of what makes for a good-looking cock, but when the ideal is looking like an eleven-year-old, that means that the old perversions have become normalized to what some might call an unhealthy extent. Though I'm not particularly inclined to jerk off to them, the eroticization of young boys has reached a point where an aesthetic and cosmetic fascism has taken hold of what illusory "community" can be said to exist. As if community were created by rainbow flags, monosyllabic club names or the generation of "sexy" handles, like godtony1986, or shaved-master, or my own, gaytrees79.

Anyway, he holds his cock like a teacup, stroking with two and sometimes three fingers, pinky set off and raised ever so slightly. The signification of feyness.

"Do you want tea with your lunch, Henry?"

"Yes. Thanks, Mom."

The claw-foot makes me imagine a house of Persian carpets and a mother drenched in pearls, doting on this kid who spends his free time jerking off for strangers on camera.

A few years ago, I heard about a pornography production class at some film school. Probably somewhere in L.A. or San Diego, because where the fuck else would they have a class like that? At the end of the semester, during final project screenings, the usual parade of films came through: girl-on-girl action with soft-focus lens, reimaginings of *Deep Throat* as tranny porn, Cinemax-style elaborate skin flicks. But the project that won accolades was the project that didn't include any sex at all, or at least nothing on camera. It was just the lens focused on two eyes, belonging to a person of indeterminate gender. It ran for ten minutes, and a lot of the students didn't get it, but the director saved the gut punch for last: the credits revealed that the entire film was shot while the subject was masturbating.

The eyes of the kid in the tub alternately focus on the camera and the task at hand. He has a smug smirk on his face that's sort of petulant and sweet. It makes me want to tousle his hair. When it starts getting somewhat more feverish, he rolls his lips into his mouth and closes his eyes, sometimes rolling them back wetly just before he does so. He's puffing up his cheeks, too. At one point, he even opens his mouth all the way, revealing these rows of perfect teeth biting very hard. Looks like the boy needs a pillow.

Just as his hand becomes blurry from the speed of his motion, the camera shifts down and back slightly, going from a longer shot of his dick, hips and torso to something broader, his inner thighs, perineum and hole coming into view in a breathtaking change of scene; long, then luscious. In my head I want the kid to be a bottom, but I also know that with a dick as big as his he'll probably always be the top.

My friend Evan always hated not knowing who he was doing porn shoots with because he couldn't prepare his ass ahead of time, and giving a stranger a condom covered in frothy lube and blood is kind of embarrassing. One time, he was the bigger one, and ended up having to fuck this desperate straight hippie kid who kept bleeding and shitting and crying, and despite all that Evan didn't lose his hard-on, because he'd been pumping Viagra all day like a good porno soldier.

Back to the kid and his perineum: it's the sort of thing I'd like to suck for hours. Like Nathan's, but more youthful. I once woke up with Nathan in a stranger's sunroom, and we were both sweating so much under this down comforter that we didn't even need lube. Just some lip-spit on the salt of the taint, and we were ready to go.

Even the pinky is wrapped around it now. The kid's stomach is contracting in that special way, trying to withhold a bit, and his eyes are going wider and then shutting for longer periods.

Apparently, a lot of people have problems with their eyes after masturbating. Take this account on the MedHelp site from someone with the handle, basar:

> *I am a 19 years old boy. I masturbate 2 or 3 times a week. Every time I masturbate it may be continue for 30 min. Nearly a year ago after a masturbating night I saw a black spot in my eye. After that every time I masturbate I see added spots and cloudy vision like floaters. And it become worse and worse every*

time. Now i have lots of them. What is the reason of creation of this floaters in realation with masturbation? What is the difference between masturbation or having sex with others that sex with others does not creat floaters? Are there any ways to treat and to avoid of creation of more floaters?

Fucking scary! But it's never happened to me, so I sort of just want to tell basar that he needs to focus on his grammar school-work and stop lying, because everyone knows that nineteen-year-olds and pretty much everyone with a dick masturbates daily until the age of forty, even fifty. Hell, your dad probably masturbates.

The tub and the kid are so white that it's almost hard to notice the spray. So quick, only five minutes of hard work! He lets go of his cock and smiles, sated, and reaches around to bring the camera closer to his stomach. There isn't really much to see—the lighting is bad—but he spreads his stuff around on his stomach and chest for a minute, seeming almost bored; drawing in the dust with a stick. The video ends.

God, that perineum.

I press PLAY again, though the screen says, *gaytrees79: You have only two free video views left today.* Whatever. I won't pay for pornography. I just want to watch the kid again. This time, I'm going to call him "Georgie."

Georgie's sitting in the tub. He probably imagines himself as a twelve-year-old, smoothed-out. He might actually be a twelve-year-old, though this site isn't the sort of place that hosts illegal images knowingly. No doubt, he's at least eighteen. A twinky eighteen.

I can hear his mother yelling at him for spending too much time in the bathroom. Nowadays, teenage boys spend as much time in the bathroom as teenage girls, according to the *Times*, beauty products lined up next to sinks. Instead of Venus, though, the boys have Axe or Swagger or Magnetic Attraction Exfoliating Enhancement Body Washizzle. I wonder if Georgie uses any of these, but the thought passes because he's starting to stroke faster, and my heels click together.

"*Oh, Georgie.*"

"*Oh, gaytrees79.*"

"*Mmm, yeahhh, Georgie.*"

"*Gaytrees79, yes yes yes, gaytrees79.*"

It's a brief James Bidgood sort of moment; I'm in the tub with him and my saliva's running all over his balls, and I have my fingers in my asshole. Georgie's holding the back of my neck. One of my hands grips the side of the tub and I start to raise myself.

Suddenly, though, his mother busts through the door. Her hair is in that very Midwestern tight bun; she's wearing a gold chain with a big fucking crucifix on it, a conservative pink blouse and mom-khakis in navy.

She screams, and it's over.

The deflation of fantasy is one of the truest routes of pleasure seeking; pursuing sexual fantasy to its logical ends makes sense, obviously, but the withholding is more rewarding. If every day of our lives was like *Pink Narcissus* or even *Fuck Me Raw: Athens Edition*, cocks would become revolting and the sweet, musty smell of butt would initiate vomiting. The mother has to interrupt, because if she didn't, everything would end in just another wadded-up tissue on my desk.

Georgie's pinky is wrapped around his dick again now, the death-grip position that means that things are about to happen. He doesn't know that this position can lead to trouble down the road, as evidenced by the countless men who write in to sex columns confessing how years of fierce-grip masturbation have made it impossible to achieve orgasm during actual sex. I whisper, "Light touches, Georgie, light touches," but he ignores me. It is hard to be ignored, even if I am alone in my room watching a screen, and so desperation is mirrored in this way. Georgie is posting videos of his svelteness to the Internet because he's teased at school for holding his Diet Coke with his pinky up, or because he does Irish dancing on the weekends, or because everyone knows what he tried to do to Keenan last summer during the camping trip. I empathize, and so we stare at each other and lick our lips and wonder about the possibilities of reaching through the screen and just holding on.

The funny thing is that if you're rich enough to have an iPhone, the possibility is already there. Grindr is an application that guys sign on to and, using GPS technology, search for other guys looking to hook up within a given radius. A former lover of mine tweeted a while back that *Grindr at the airport makes U look at EVERY1 diffrrntly*. I can only imagine, because iPhones kind of scare the fuck out of me, and evidently, Grindr scares the fuck out of the Apple corporation, as they're trying to ban it from their app store.

I love Georgie's stomach contracting and expanding. My friend Myles is a chubby chaser, and I've always wanted to ask him whether he gets off on the stomach thing, too, or whether there's some sort of impossibility there. I've even done it with bigger guys, in claw-foot bathtubs no less, but I cannot remember whether there was the same level of gasping and shuddering as with the skinnier types I usually go for—ribs showing themselves, the abdomen tightening, relaxinging, tightening.

Georgie's almost done. His mother's calling him for dinner.

Maybe he'll eat in silence, his kid sister babbling at his parents while they wonder what they're going to do with him. Maybe he'll go out afterward, saying he's going to meet friends, but just walk in the park alone. Maybe he'll loiter around the toilets, waiting for the inevitable stranger to wander up, lead him into a stall and suck him off in three of the best minutes of his life. Maybe the stranger will give Georgie his number, and Georgie will throw it away in a panic before laundry day. Maybe.

It's strange how he smiles for the camera. It's not a seductive smile, really, but the sort of smile one would give for a family vacation photograph taken at the beach, posing alongside little sister, Natalia, and Mom and Dad with Atlantic waves crashing and spreading behind them. Georgie's the tallest next to the patriarch, his clavicle winging out beneath his neck. The smile isn't forced, because everyone loves being at the beach, but there's a quality of it that says, "I belong somewhere else." To smile like this in a video on a porn site seems ludicrous, but it's just a wank piece, so Georgie can do whatever he wants and I'll understand. I'm sitting in my room, my cock wet and hanging out of my briefs, my fingers pressed against my prostate.

I wish I had an iPhone.

BODIES IN MOTION

Johnny Murdoc

Two weeks before school started, I went to teacher orientation and found myself staring at Nathan Derricks, the new assistant coach. Nathan wasn't new to me. Eight years ago, we both attended this very high school. He was on the football team. Everyone in school knew him. Almost everyone in school wanted to be with him. Including me. He was that guy.

In a small town, teacher orientation is something of a class reunion. Most everyone runs away from his high school, his hometown, but some of us come back. We become the teachers; the parents; the ones who couldn't stay away.

There's Marcia Tungsten, who wrote every boy's name on her binder with a heart around it well into high school: music teacher. Bill Dyson, who played guitar in the quad to a small circle of tone-deaf groupies: English teacher. Davie Strunk, former bully who I had a crush on even after he slammed me into my locker: sociology teacher. Carol Jacobs, who used to give blow jobs beneath the bleachers to anyone who would take his dick out in front of her. I should know, because she gave me one. She's the school nurse now. Then there's Nathan.

And me. I was a nobody, and now I'm a science teacher.

Over the summer, I grew my beard out. It makes me look older and, I think, more teacher-like. Students have a hard time paying attention to someone who looks more like an older brother than a teacher. So I grew the beard, and I let my dark hair grow longer than usual, so that it curls. I've been fighting the curls all my life, but for now I let them go.

"Are you married?" my students ask me.

"No," I say, not lying.

"Do you have a girlfriend?" they ask.

"No," I say, not lying.

To class, I wear a dress shirt and a sports coat. I'm a high school teacher wearing college professor drag. During the day, I lose the jacket, and I roll my sleeves up. I talk loudly, but I give my students a chance to speak, as well. I do my best to bring science to them not as an idea in a textbook but as a set of rules for questioning.

"Who is that man in that picture?" a student asks, pointing to the framed portrait on my desk. "He your dad?"

"No. That's Carl Sagan," I say.

"Who's Carl Sagan?" he asks.

"He's the reason I love science," I say.

After fourth period, I duck into the break room, hoping to have the place to myself. Instead, sitting at the table in the middle of the room, I find Nathan Derricks.

"Hey, Johnson," he says, calling me by my last name.

"Nathan," I say. Nathan Derricks has never said more than four words to me in my life.

"How's it going?" he asks. Seven words, now.

"Good," I say, turning my back to him, somehow instinctively wanting him to leave me alone. Eight years later, and I fall back into the nerd roll, casting Derricks in the jock role. I focus on pouring coffee into my mug. The coffee is several hours old and smells like it.

As I stir in a packet of sugar, I realize that Derricks is standing directly behind me. He sits his coffee cup next to mine.

"Johnson, I've been meaning to ask you something," he says.

"What's up?"

"I was wondering—"

"Yeah?"

"All those rumors back in high school: were they true?" My heart thumps hard in my chest. Did I really come back to school just so that I could get bullied again?

I take a couple of deep breaths, try to calm down. "Which rumors would those be, Nathan?"

"That you were gay."

I don't say anything.

"If so, then I bet you had a pretty big hard-on for me, didn't you? All the girls did."

I turn to face him. He's standing only inches away, practically on top of me. I breathe in, replacing the smell of burnt coffee with the smell of Nathan Derricks: sweat and deodorant. My dick thickens in my pants. "Nate," I say, "what are you talking about?"

"I'm just curious," he says. Did he just move in closer?

"That was a long time ago." I sidestep him and manage to avoid bumping into him as he makes half a gesture to stand in my way.

I leave the break room without saying anything else.

That night, in my empty apartment, I masturbate without looking at porn for the first time in years.

* * *

In the mornings, I get to work early and run the track. Occasionally other staff members are there, but aside from a friendly nod we don't really speak to each other. We're not here for work. Running laps, I can clear my mind, stop thinking and revel in the feeling of my heart racing and my muscles burning. Summer is cooling its way into fall.

I do my best to avoid crossing paths with Nathan. It's not hard. I steal coffee refills between classes and avoid the teachers' lounge on my free hour. His few academic classes are in another wing, and he spends most of his time in the gym. I spent years learning how to avoid certain people in these halls. I'm something of a professional, now.

"Were you a student here?" a student asks.

"Yeah," I say.

"Did you like it here back then?"

"Does anyone like high school while they're in it?"

At the end of September, Principal Lohbeck and Superintendent Lowell call another mandatory meeting to discuss the football season and the homecoming dance. Dozens of teachers fill the high school cafeteria, splintering into cliques as impenetrable as those formed by the students during the day. Against the far wall are a coffeemaker and a box of stale doughnuts, like we're in an AA meeting. I sit and try to pay attention in a way that suggests I'm not interested in doing anything but. Nathan is sitting at a table not far from me, though, and it's hard not to be aware of him. He sits with the athletic department.

After the meeting, I shuffle paperwork back into my briefcase and stand. Not far from the door, a small circle of people I can't help but recognize has formed. Marcia, the lovelorn music teacher; Bill, the prematurely balding former rock star; Davie, the sociopathic sociology teacher; Carol, the nurse with cock-sucker lips; and Nathan. Marcia waves at me, urging me to join them. I try not to, but I'm like a meteor that can't avoid the Earth's gravity. I'm like the Moon.

"We should all go for drinks after work," Marcia is saying. The group nods, agreeing with her. Carol looks at Nathan like she wants to duck behind the bleachers. Nathan smiles at me. I try to avoid looking him in the eyes.

"I can't believe we haven't gotten together before this," Carol says. It's unclear whether she's talking to all of us or just Nathan.

"I know," Marcia says. It appears that if anyone's going to stand in the way of my avoiding a high school reunion, it's her. "I can't go anywhere tonight, but what do you say we go out for happy hour on Friday night? I bet we all have so much to catch up on and so many stories."

"Can't on Friday nights," Nathan said. "Football."

Carol pouted.

"But maybe some weeknight?"

The group nods in agreement, and I fake a smile and excuse myself.

In the parking lot, I walk determinedly toward my car. As I stop to find my key, a hand falls on my shoulder.

"Where are you rushing off to?" It's Nathan, of course.

"Home," I say.

"Oh, to your boyfriend?"

"No."

"I thought you might like to go get a drink. You know, without the reunion."

We would have actually had to be a union for it to be a reunion. "I have a lot of papers," I say. "To grade."

"C'mon, Johnson. Papers can wait. Let's grab a beer."

"Sorry. I can't, really. Maybe another time."

Nathan stares at me, squints his eyes a little as though that will help him figure me out.

"Excuse me," I say, nodding back at my car. Nathan steps closer and his chest presses against mine. He pushes me back until my ass is against the car door. He kisses me. Presses his body against mine, his hips against mine.

"I just want to have a little fun with you," he says.

"I have to go home," I say.

On the drive home, my heart is beating loudly. I can feel my blood race through my veins. My cock is hard. At home, I don't grade papers. I can barely make it in the door before I'm pulling my cock free from my khakis. I think about Nathan's five o'clock shadow; the definition of his chest beneath his shirt; his smirk and his inquisitive eyes; the force of his crotch pressing against mine.

I ejaculate, kneeling on my living room floor, spraying cum onto my work shirt.

It takes extra time on the track for me to put it all together. As much as I try to think about anything else, I think only of Nathan. I had assumed, incorrectly, that Nathan's actions toward me in the past month or so had been intended to antagonize me, to bring up old memories. Revisiting those days, despite voluntarily choosing to return to my own high school, is something I have no interest in doing.

So, it begs the question: why am I not interested? Ten years ago, twelve years ago, I was in love with Nathan Derricks. He wasn't ever the only one. I never had any fairy-tale dreams about him. He was one of the ones, though. I used to sit in the locker room after gym class, taking my time getting undressed, showered and dressed. The more time I spent there, the more chances I had to catch a glimpse of someone naked.

The more chances I had to realize that I would never have them.

The fact is, Nathan represents everything I have been attracted to since the day that I've been able to find anyone attractive. Simultaneously, he's everyone I've grown to resent because I can't have them.

I run every morning and some evenings. Most teachers put on weight as the school year progresses. They're busy grading papers and stressed out. They spend more time snacking, less time taking care of themselves. I don't. I run more, and more, and more. I lose weight. I tone up. I didn't look this good when I was in high school.

"I didn't take you for a runner," Nathan says one morning, appearing beside me on the track. I hadn't even noticed anyone on the track, let alone heard him come up behind me.

"You don't know anything about me," I say.

"It's not for lack of trying." He keeps pace with me easily. I try to see as much of him as I can out of the corner of my eye, without being too obvious. He's still in good shape, his white cotton T-shirt clinging nicely to his torso. His body is a little softer than it was in high school, though, and he's starting to show hints of love handles. He's wearing short jogging shorts, and it takes me a couple of glances to recognize something: he's not wearing underwear, or a jock strap. With each step we take, his dick flops around in his shorts. I can't help but look. My cock responds, stiffening in my briefs.

I look up and realize that Nathan is watching me. Watching me watch his dick. He smiles; no, smirks.

I look ahead, try to focus on running. I'm on my fourth mile. I want to keep running until Nathan breaks off, heads to the showers; leaves me alone. Fat chance. I run. The laps add up. Nathan isn't even breathing hard. My chest is burning. I run until I can't, and then I break off for the locker room. The track is at the bottom of the hill, and I feel like going up it will kill me but I do.

The locker room is empty, and every sound is the loudest sound in the room. Each sound bounces off of concrete and metal lockers and tiles and echoes until it is swallowed by the next sound. I undress, hoping to shower and get out of here quickly, get to class.

I hang my towel up and step into the shower room. Ten metal spigots stick out of the walls. Between each one a plastic soap dispenser is mounted on the wall. I pick a showerhead near the entryway. I twist the tap and I can hear water knocking through the pipes behind the wall. It's loud but it doesn't cover up the sounds of the locker room. I shampoo my hair and rinse, the water sliding over my ears and filling my head with the sound of rain. Still, I hear a locker slamming closed. I turn to the spigot and let the water slap my face. I am not alone. I run my hand over my face and open my eyes, and Nathan is standing across from me. His body is turned to me, his head titled back as he wets his hair and rubs his hands over his face, and I can't avoid seeing his body and his muscles and his cock. His body is hairier than I thought it would be. His cock is more normal than I thought it would be. It isn't the giant jock cock that I had fantasized about when I was younger. It is a cock though, a cock attached to a naked man who I had fantasized about, had loved and hated and tried to avoid but is now standing in front of me. My own cock responds. I turn my back to him.

"What do I have to do to get you to pay attention to me?" he asks.

* * *

I consider masturbating in the staff bathroom on my break, but then I imagine Mr. Douglas, my ninth-grade math teacher, doing the same years before, before his heart attack made him the bottom half of a fraction. I think about his thick fist pounding his cock at lightning speed as his fat belly hangs over arm. I never saw Mr. Douglas naked, but it's frighteningly easy to imagine, and I lose the urge to follow in his footsteps by masturbating at work.

Still, the image of Nathan's cock floats in my head all day long—his nice, surprisingly normal cock. I welcome the distractions of my day: the teaching, the presentations. It's the quiet moments when he's there: study time and my free hour. I sit at my desk, my head propped up on my hands, and I think about Nathan Derricks naked. It's no longer just the fantasy of Nathan Derricks, the hyperfantasy version of Nathan Derricks that I've been living with but the real Nathan Derricks: His hairy stomach. His wide feet and wide toenails. His armpit hair. His—

"Applebee's, six o'clock tomorrow night," Marcia Tungsten says, sticking her head through the doorway of my classroom.

"What?" I ask.

"You remember," she says. "We all agreed to go out for drinks."

"Oh, I, uh—"

"Nonsense," she says. "The whole gang'll be there. It'll be just like old times!"

Just like old times. Great.

I sit in my car in the Applebee's parking lot for five minutes. I try to talk myself out of going in. I'm reaching up to start my car when someone knocks on my window. I jump and drop my keys. Marcia is standing right outside, waving. Her hand moves like a hummingbird wing, a quick fleshy blur of excitement. I force a smile, and then she points at the restaurant. I nod at her, and I hear her say, "I'll see you in there!" through the glass. I nod again. When she disappears, I let my head fall and hit the steering wheel.

The Applebee's looks like it always does: like a high school reunion with middle-aged people standing around drinking too much and trying too hard to impress one another, laughing too loudly. For a moment I'm ashamed that I could be confused with someone who would choose to be here.

My own small high school reunion is sitting around a large circular table near the back of the restaurant. Marcia is already drinking from a comically large margarita. It would be funny if it weren't so sad. She waves at me when I approach the table, that same spastic hummingbird wave.

"Scootch in there next to Nathan," she says as I approach the table. Nathan is sitting on the outermost side of table. He smiles at me. It is not the smile he has for everyone else here. He pats the seat next to him as he slides over, making room for me.

We order. The food comes. Beneath the table, I feel Nathan's hand on my thigh. I didn't think he would try anything in front of everyone. I kick his shoe beneath the table and he smiles at me. His hand squeezes my thigh. His hand feels good. After my plate is clean and I'm rushing to finish my second beer because I want to leave, Nathan gets brave and his hand goes from my thigh to my crotch. I kick him hard enough to jolt the table. Everyone looks at me.

After a moment Marcia says, "Well, then. Is everyone excited about homecoming?" She seems like she genuinely is. Nathan smiles.

I'm decidedly less than excited about homecoming. Mr. Woods, the head of the science department, backed out of chaperoning at the last minute. "Barb's mother isn't doing so well," he said. "She's ninety-five years old, and at that age every little thing could be *the* thing, if you know what I mean." I did know what he meant. He was using the sick grandmother story on me, which is probably some kind of hellish karma coming back at me for doing the same thing to him when he was my health teacher. I hate high school.

"What do you say, Mr. Derricks?" Carol Jacobs asks, beaming at Nathan. "You boys going to win the big game on Friday?" It hits me that it was actually at our senior year homecoming game that she went down on me. I had a date for the dance the next night, Susie Sanders, but I still let Carol suck my dick. I can't remember what I was thinking about when I came in her mouth, but it wasn't her and it wasn't Susie Sanders. It very well could have been Nathan Derricks.

"I think we've got a pretty good chance," Nathan says. "The boys are doing good this season."

"Go Warriors!" Marcia says.

I can't think of anywhere I'd rather be less than homecoming, the game or the dance. Except maybe here, at Applebee's.

On Friday night the Westfield Warriors do win their game, and the dance on Saturday is all the more boisterous for it. The student body is charged, excited and filled with school spirit in a way that I remember being vaguely infectious but now only fills me with dread as I'm taxed with keeping students in line. For the most part, the evening goes well. Here or there a couple has to be told to maintain boundaries, and a fight breaks out between two football players, each claiming responsibility for the prior night's victory.

I do my best to remain a wallflower. The evening feels much like my own homecoming dance did. Even though Susie Sanders had come as my date she had spent most of the evening dancing with her friends. It is entirely possible that she had picked up on my lack of actual romantic interest in her, or it could have been that my friend Billy had told a few friends that Carol Jacobs went down on me and those few friends had told enough people that it was likely that Susie Sanders had found out. If there was anything a teenage girl loved more than having a date for the dance, it was having a reason to hate her date so that she and her friends could revel in the drama. That could be an unfair assessment, but this homecoming dance now is doing nothing to disprove the theory as I watch small mobs gather around the two girls left behind when their football player boyfriends were asked to leave after the aforementioned fight. History repeats itself and nowhere can a better example be found than at a high school dance.

"It's like watching tiny versions of ourselves, isn't it?" Nathan Derricks is standing next to me. I didn't see him come in or come near me, but he's here now and he looks good. He's wearing something close to formal attire. He smells good. For a brief moment I want him to invite me to dance.

"Johnson," he says.

"Derricks," I say. "Congratulations on the game."

"Thanks," he says. "The guys deserve this dance."

"Too bad it's not a dance for us, huh?"

"Too bad, yeah. I can think of other ways to celebrate, though."

I step out of the gymnasium and cross the hall to the boys' room. I'm not surprised to smell faint hints of pot, but the restroom is empty now. As I step up to the urinal and unzip my pants the door opens and Nathan follows me in. He takes the urinal right next to mine. There is no divider. His arm touches mine. I do my best to stare straight forward. There's no way I'll be able to piss so I stand there for a moment, then I shake my dick and stuff it back into my pants. I step up to the sink and glance back at Nathan, half expecting to see him jerking off but he's actually pissing, so I look down at my own hands as I wash them. Nathan flushes and steps up next to me, washes his hands. He looks at me in the mirror.

"Am I doing something wrong, Johnson?" he asks. I cock an eyebrow. I don't know what to say to him. He doesn't wait for me to respond. "I know I can be kind of a cocky asshole. Shit, I spent four years in this school where everyone gave me everything I ever wanted, so sometimes I can't help it."

He turns to face me. "Maybe you like it romantic, though. Should I be sending you flowers? Leaving little cards in your mailbox? I don't know, I always thought you'd like it a little more aggressive." He takes a step toward me and I take a step back. The off-white concrete blocks of the restroom are right behind me. Nathan steps closer. "Tell me, Johnson, do you want it sweet and romantic, or do you want it rough?"

I want to tell him that I don't want it at all, but I'd be lying. "...Rough."

Nathan pushes me against the wall next to the hand dryer. He presses his mouth to mine and I can taste a hint of beer. I open my mouth to him and he pushes his crotch against mine. His dick is hard. His tongue is thick and forceful in my mouth and I relax against the concrete wall, letting Nathan take control. He slides a hand beneath my jacket and rubs my chest through my dress shirt. He grunts into my mouth and thrusts his crotch against me. His dick, so normal the other day, feels huge and hard and hot against my thigh. Nathan slides a hand down my chest and pulls at my belt buckle.

I place a hand against his chest and break our kiss. "You

know I'm not going to have sex with you in the boys' bathroom, right?"

"But you are going to have sex with me?" Nathan raises an eyebrow, and I can't help but smile at him.

We duck out of the bathroom and into the hallway. Nathan takes my hand and pulls me along. It feels like we're sixteen again, hoping that no one catches us.

In the locker room I expect Nathan to head for his office, but he slams me against the lockers. The metal clangs loudly, amplified by the cold, concrete emptiness of the space. Nathan kisses my neck and his body is warm against mine. He pulls his jacket off and lets it fall to the floor as he continues to kiss—no, suck—at my neck. I grab at his head, my fingers sliding through his hair, and I push him harder against my skin. His hands pull at my jacket and shirt and grope my dick through my pants. His mouth covers mine. He kisses like he can't get enough, like he would swallow me if he could. Music vibrates through the walls. A stairwell and a few doors are all that separate us from the gymnasium.

Nathan is determined in a way that no lover of mine has ever been. He pulls open my shirt and lifts my undershirt, exposing my skin. He continues his wet, leeching kisses down my chest and falls to his knees. My nipples harden into tight little nubs, either from the cool air or the wave of sensation rippling through me as Nathan drags his lips across my skin.

He wraps his mouth around my cock through the fabric of my pants. My dick is hard and sore, and I want it to be free. I want it to be in his mouth. He rubs his face against my crotch and inhales deeply. He pops the button on my pants with one hand and yanks them open. My cock fights against my boxers, a thin fleshy stripe visible through the open slit. Nathan tucks his fingers into my waistband and yanks everything down, pooling my boxers and my pants around my ankles. My dick, hard and now free, smacks against his face and he smiles up at me.

Nathan swallows my entire cock in one smooth move, and it occurs to me that this is not the first time he's done this. He wraps his hand around the base of my dick and squeezes as he slides his head back. He looks up at me like he adores me. If he had just made that face earlier, we would have been here much sooner. Then again, most people do look more appealing to me with my dick in their mouth.

Nathan lets my cock fall from his mouth and looks up at me. "Turn around," he says.

"What?"

"Turn around." Nathan places his hands on my hips and tugs until I comply and turn my back to him. He grabs an asscheek in each hand, and I feel his mouth on one cheek and then the other, his kisses leaving small circular spreads of saliva behind. His nose traces up my asscrack and he kisses again, this time at the very top of the split, and I feel his tongue slide out and taste my skin. My knees waver. Nathan pulls my asscheeks apart and exposes my crack to the cool air. He buries his face there and his tongue pokes at my hole. I push my hips back and he responds by digging in farther. I gasp, my face pressed hard against the cold metal of the locker in front of me. Nathan licks and probes and penetrates me with his tongue. He eats at my ass with all of the aggression of his kisses, with the aggression of his attitude and his come-ons. He eats my ass like he wants to conquer it.

Nathan stands quickly and smacks my ass, hard. He presses his body against mine before I can protest, and his dick, hard and exposed—he must have freed it while he was rimming me— slides between my asscheeks. He kisses and sucks at the back of my neck.

"Did you like that?" he asks.

"Yeah," I gasp. "Yeah."

Nathan thrusts against me, his cock rising and cresting out of my crack, and my hips push forward. My hard cock smacks into the locker, and I look down to see a string of precum bridge my dick and the dull green metal.

"Can I fuck you?" Nathan asks.

"Do you have a condom?" I ask.

"Two," he says. "I brought two."

"I want to suck your dick," I say. I want to suck his dick, I want to eat his ass, I want to fuck him. I want to cuddle with him. I want to punch him.

"No time for that now." I feel his hand slide into my crack and his finger press against my hole. Above us, the music shifts from slow dance to rock music. Nathan bites my shoulder and then licks my earlobe.

"Fuck me," I say.

"Yeah?"

"Fuck me."

Nathan steps away for a moment, and I feel cold and alone but only briefly. He moves fast. I look over my shoulder to see him quickly shedding his clothes and pulling a condom wrapper from his pants pocket. When he stands again his cock is erect and huge, hard enough that it barely waves as he moves. He tears open the condom package and pulls out a flesh-colored rubber. I watch him unroll it over his dick. He smiles at me and I think of a saying I read once: *In nature, a smile is just another show of teeth*.

Nathan steps behind me again and wraps a hand around my chest. He hugs me tightly. I reach behind me and grasp his cock, which feels impossibly big. The condom is prelubricated, but I want something more.

"Spit on it," I say, pulling my hand away. "On the condom."

Nathan does and he strokes his cock. I grab him again and pull him toward me. I push his dick down until it lines up with my hole. He's so hard that his dick resists being pushed down. "Go slow."

I push back against him as he presses against me. I do my best to relax, and Nathan's dick slides into my hole a little. I am slick and open from his rim job, and it doesn't hurt like I'm afraid it will. I push back more until it feels like he's halfway in, and I keep my hand on his cock to keep him from going too far. He tightens his grip on my chest and then pulls his dick back a little, sliding back out. I realize then that it's the opposite of what I want, that I want him inside of me, entirely. Completely. I push back against him and release my grip on his erection. I slide my hand around his midsection and grab his ass, pulling him close to me. He slides in completely, pubes to ass. He exhales and his breath is warm on my neck and ear.

"That good?" he asks.

I bite my lip and nod. I grunt. It's all I have. He pumps against me, once, trying to go in farther, and my dick jumps. He grabs my nipple in between his thumb and forefinger and pinches hard. The feeling is sharp, like a piercing. I grunt again and Nathan fucks me. I keep one arm in front of me, forearm against the lockers, and I stroke my dick with the other hand. I go slowly, the feeling of his dick in my ass and his fingers pinching my nipple so intense that I won't last long if I move too quickly. Nathan kisses my neck, bites my shoulder and whispers in my ear. "You like that," he says. It's not a question. "Yeah," he says. He presses his sweaty face against my skin as he pumps in and out. He lets go of my nipple and slaps his hand against my chest. My skin stings in a line from where his hand and arm cut across my chest. My knees buckle but Nathan holds me up. He holds me close to him, his chest flat against my back.

He fucks and he slaps and he bites and he kisses and I cum. I try to hold it back but I can't. I squeeze my dick and grunt and long, ropey shots streak out toward the lockers, splashing against the green metal. Nathan laughs and slams his cock into me, holding it in as my orgasm causes my asshole to pucker around his dick. I cum like I haven't in a long time; my shots are hard and straight and thick, the white liquid stark against the painted locker. Nathan wraps his hand over mine and helps me stroke myself. His grip is firm and I know this is what it feels like to be conquered. To say that it's anything else would be a lie.

As my cum slows and starts to drip rather than spray Nathan resumes his fucking. The feeling of his dick slamming inside of me is completely different now than it was before, my skin so much more sensitive. I brace myself against the locker, looking down at my own semen sliding down it. Nathan grabs me by the hips and thrusts, no longer concerned with how I feel. He doesn't last long, though. His grip tightens on my hips, and he buries himself as deeply as he can, and I feel his dick throb inside of me. He grunts now, loud, and then shivers. His grunt grows into something louder and longer, almost a victory yell, not out of place here in the locker room, even if it has nothing to do with sports.

After his orgasm subsides his knees shake and he pulls himself out of my ass. His chest is heaving and he's smiling. He squats and then falls back to sit on the bare concrete floor. His erection, still wrapped in the condom and still hard, points upward. A pouch of white cum hangs from the tip. "Fuck," he says. I sit down next to him. The floor is cold but I want to touch him, hold him. He puts an arm around my shoulder and I look at him. He's nude except for his socks. My own clothes are draping off my shoulders or wrapped around my ankles.

"Lie back," he says and I do. We could be anywhere, but

we're not. We're lying on the floor of the locker room at West-field High. Nathan's chest is rising and falling quickly; I put my shoulder on it and look down as his cock deflates, drifting to one side as though the load of cum still hanging in the condom is dragging it down.

"We're really terrible chaperones," Nathan says and we both laugh. Lying here on the cold floor of the locker room while the homecoming dance continues above our heads feels preposterous and right and good. Everything about this school year feels preposterous and right and good.

Everything feels good for now.

SAVING TOBIAS

Jeff Mann

for Tiffany Trent

Tobias Crockett has good taste in accommodations. The Tabard Inn is quaint and historic, full of antiques, paintings and well-heeled sorts chattering over meals and cocktails. All a bit noisy for me, an undead introvert accustomed to the high, forested silence of West Virginia's Potomac Highlands, so I'm sitting as far away from people as possible, here in a dark corner of the parlor. The ceiling's low and dark-beamed, like the Cape Cod tavern where I used to hunt in the midseventies. Tonight's February gusty, so the big fireplace is in use, flame-light flickering over glossy wood-paneled walls. The few table lamps are turned low, creating an atmosphere of dim intimacy: perfect for sipping red wine and studying Tobias across the room.

His name befits him. *Tobias.* It's Hebrew for "God is good." God has been good to him indeed. So far. Handsome blond giant, wealthy, talented, powerful, he's as magnificent as

Oedipus must have been a few hours before the truth, before the kingly fool thrust the pin of his mother's brooch, his wife's brooch, into his eyes. The truth can do that, certainly. Put out the eyes, splinter the soul, castrate, eviscerate, shatter. The truth is what I bring tonight.

I've had my sights on Tobias for several years now. But with immortality to enjoy, why rush the consummation of a passion? Back during his country-music days, he was one of few men who brought out the bottom in me. His bulk and rough rebel persona were the reasons, I think. I would examine the images on his CD covers—blond goatee, blue eyes, pouty lips, cowboy hat—and wish he were on top of me thrusting away. When I attended his concerts with my country-boy lover Matt, who's an enthusiast of all things Nashville, I'd watch Tobias swagger the stage, finger his guitar, gift us with that resonant baritone and those macho bad-boy lyrics and imagine him pushing me over a sawhorse and ramming me with the yee-haw vigor of the Virginia farm boy he used to be. It would be a heady pleasure to be filled up by a man that burly, that much bigger than I. I might even let him come inside me before I turned on him and put him in his place.

But Tobias has, alas, put music behind him for politics. That's his fatal misstep, his *hamartia*, as Aristotle put it when analyzing *Oedipus*. That's what he's doing in DC tonight: using the good looks and charisma that made him a country-music superstar to network with Republican hangers-on and syco- phants; a long way from his Wytheville roots, his glamorous years in Nashville. Now he's a member of Virginia's General Assembly, a busy senator moving back and forth between Rich- mond and Washington, a power broker planning the move from state to national politics. The five middle-aged men sitting with him and guffawing by the fire are probably congressmen. All quite wealthy, judging by the cut of their business suits. And all right-wingers, no doubt of that.

My handsome Tobias should have stuck to songwriting. If he had, the fantasies I entertained about him wouldn't have shifted so radically and moved into the sphere of practical planning. I wouldn't be here tonight, only yards away, admiring his face and body, sipping this cabernet, readying the scourge.

What a fine specimen he is. He leans back in his leather-upholstered chair, drinking beer, grinning at some colleague's joke. His eyes are as blue as the photos on his CDs. He has a full head of curly blond hair, and his goatee is golden brown and carefully trimmed, bespeaking carefully controlled wildness. His lips are very full, the lower one so thick it contributes to the surly look he's know for in the press, a pout made all the more dramatic-dark by the rare gleam of his arrogant smiles. The jeans and muscle-shirts of his Nashville days have been replaced by slick politico suits, though he has yet to relinquish his cowboy hats and boots, just to retain the good-ole-boy image that appeals to so many of his conservative constituents. Expert at studying clothed male physiques and discerning how those forms might look stripped bare, I can make out the wide shoulders, thick chest and beer belly of a well-fed ex-athlete. At his age, midforties, the bulk's as much fat as it is muscle, a proportion that has always appealed to me, bear aficionado that I am. Big as he is, he'll keep me snug and warm tonight, after our official meeting.

My kind—Scots Highlanders, mountain men—we love to tell stories. I order a second glass of wine from a lean young waiter with hairy forearms and an angular Mediterranean face shadowed with beard—a muskily aromatic boy who, due to my plans for Tobias, will be spared my sharp attentions tonight—and I think about those whose stories brought me here. Karen,

Charlotte, sweet little Chet: three of my handsome senator's
ill-fated constituents. Vivid narrative often makes for the most
convincing political advice. Once Tobias retires for the night,
we'll begin that summit discussion.

As if on cue, Tobias checks his watch, orders a bourbon
nightcap, knocks it back, and says goodnight to his little crew
of sartorial vipers. It's approaching midnight, and he has early
morning meetings, he explains. No distant human ear could
pick out his words over the chatter of the parlor, but I can. I can
smell him too. As he passes me, heading for his room, he leaves
a lingering scent of spicy aftershave, and the sweat-smell of a big
man whose deodorant gave out by late afternoon. I lick my lips.
Beneath the table, I nudge my hardening cock with the back of
my thumb. He will, without a doubt, taste as fine as he smells.

I have had several hundred years to learn the subtleties of
strategy, and so I wait for a bit once Tobias leaves. After what
will happen to him tonight, I don't want anyone remembering
me as a suspicious character who directly followed him out.
Instead, I finish my wine slowly. I think of Karen walking into
the barn, Chet standing by the creek, Charlotte gasping in the
hospital bed. I study the waiter, whose shirt is open one flirtatious button too many to be truly professional, and I make out,
in the cleft his open collar makes, the black chest hair I've tasted
on so many Middle-Eastern, Italian and Greek men. Perhaps,
upon my next trip to DC, I will have to sample him, though
carefully and abstemiously, considering his frail build. With
a man as hefty as Tobias, my appetites will have significantly
wider range.

It is time. Leaving my asocial nook, I stand by the fire to take
in the heat and finish that last sip of wine. Cold as I am, cold
since 1730, I gravitate to fireplaces, to any flame, those restless
substitutes for the sunlight I am denied. Matt, sweet husbear,

pants away summer afternoons stripped to the waist, chopping oak to fill the woodshed, and by the time I rise with dusk, he is richly rank and tastes of sweat-salt all over. With those hard-won cords of wood, he keeps the hearths hot all winter in our snow-swathed Mount Storm farmhouse. Every night, as hard wind rattles the panes, he fixes us hot scotch toddies, strips us both and pulls me into bed to curl with him beneath the quilts. He wraps his big arms around me, presses his hot, hairy chest and belly against mine and sighs, head lolling dreamily, as I carefully and blissfully feed on him. Sweet boy, he has never entirely reconciled himself to what happens when my rages and my hungers go untrammeled, but he certainly understands my need for erotic and culinary variety, and, as grief stricken as he's been lately—sobbing on my shoulder every night for a week—I think he understands the necessity of this mission I'm on tonight. The nation, after all, stands in need of improvement.

Outside the Tabard, thickening snowflakes scurry down N Street like swarms of white flies. In order to visit Tobias with complete discretion, I must indulge in a little shapeshifting. That's the ability that Matt has always most envied in me, ever since he found out what I really was, a wintry night much like this one, down by Kanawha Falls. My paranormal powers delight him, especially when I gently pluck his adorable, furry mass into my claws, spread my wings and give him a ride up to the top of Spruce Knob to take in the summer stars.

So, were there onlookers—and there are not—they might see, striding into tonight's dark DC alley, a tall man dressed in a long black Western duster, sporting unruly, gray-streaked hair and a silver beard. They might see, flying out of the alley, an unnaturally large, hoary-backed, black-winged bat, a bat that methodically hovers by window after window of the Tabard Inn, front and back, looking for ingress, some escape from the cold. To those hypothetical witnesses, the size of the bat would be odd enough; odder still, its presence in midwinter, when it should be hibernating.

Here is Tobias, in a top-floor room in the back of the inn. He's chosen it for its spacious privacy, its relative isolation, desires that conveniently dovetail with my intentions tonight. I perch on the sill, swaying in the cold wind, hungry darkness on the edge of the light, savoring the warmth so soon to come. He's pulled off his blazer and tie, unbuttoned his dress shirt a few notches and rolled up his sleeves. The light of a single lamp glints along his forearm fur. He sits at the desk, big fingers working over his laptop. He uncaps a bottle of scotch, fills a water glass with its amber, slugs it down and sets out his clothes for tomorrow's meetings.

And then Tobias strips for me. Not that he knows he has an audience. He stands, tugs his shirt over his head and tosses it on the couch. He pulls off one cowboy boot, then, hopping around, pulls off the other. He unzips his charcoal-gray slacks, shucks them and his boxers down his thick, hairy thighs. For a few seconds, as if aware he has an admirer, he stands naked in front of an ornately framed antique mirror. His back to the window in which I peer, he grins at himself, knowing his power. He grins and lifts his glass to his own reflection. The world is his. His charm knows no limits. Tonight, he sleeps only five blocks from the White House, but in the future, perhaps...

Tobias is built just as my careful study of him in the parlor led me to believe. In the mirror's depths loom his huge foot- ball player's shoulders, his chunky pecs, his solid, muscled arms. Only a little blond hair around his nipples and over his sternum, to my disappointment, though there's a decent thatch across his tastily broad, gone-to-seed beer belly, honey-blond fur the color of broom sedge that whispers over abandoned pastures back in

Appalachia. His back, turned to me, is wide and muscled; his ass is beefy, smooth, curvaceous and very pale. It will feel like volcanic velvet beneath my cheek. He's the perfect combination of occasional weight lifting—my guess is his ego demands that he stay in some kind of shape—and regular gastronomic indulgence; a poor boy who grows up to live high on the hog just can't forego good food and drink.

Ripe, ripe, mature, ripe. Other than the sad sparseness of his chest hair, he's exactly my type.

The proud gentleman from Virginia gulps the last of the glass and steps into the bathroom, beyond the line of my sight. There's the rush and splash of the shower; wafts of steam curl around the frame of the bathroom door.

Time to focus. My membranous darkness and silvery fur dissolve. As glowing chartreuse mist, I hover about the window, find a slight opening between brick and frame—these old buildings are always blessed with expedient little gaps—and enter. Time for Tobias's surprise.

By the time tonight's lover has finished his shower, I'm naked too, cozy coverlet pulled up to my belly, propped up on thick pillows, hands behind my head. If he were gay, he might perhaps—if he were into leatherbears instead of twinks—enjoy the sight of me, my thick beard, my hairy chest and armpits, my tattoos. But he's straight—a nasty homophobe, in fact—and besides, it takes him a few seconds to notice, in the low light, the silent stranger awaiting him. Oblivious, he fumbles about for his robe in a closet at the other end of the large room, pulls it on, belts it, pours himself another shot of scotch and then turns toward the bed.

If I were in his shoes—well, his situation, I should say, since he's barefoot—I might drop the glass in shock. He doesn't. He simply gasps. He tightens his grip on his drink and, born fighter, starts assessing. You can tell from his song lyrics that he was quite the redneck bar-brawler in his day. He's bigger than I am, he figures out fast. I'm naked, I have no weapons in sight. His initial second of fear metamorphoses almost instantly into anger.

Tobias backs up a step and says, low, intense, "Who the fuck are *you?*"

I smile. I stare into his wide blue eyes and start feeling for a purchase in his thoughts. He shakes his head and takes another step back.

"Bad manners, Senator Crockett. Aren't you going to offer me a drink?" I arch luxuriously against the flannel sheet, run my fingers through my silver chest hair, and keep smiling. "I prefer single malt, but I'll settle for that blended you have there."

Two more steps back, then three to the left, and he's put the scotch on a dresser and pulled a gun out of his suitcase. *That does it,* he thinks. *Checkmate. I was born to take control.*

"I asked you a question. Who the hell are you? And why the *fuck* are you here?" Tobias levels the gun at me. I level my glance at him. I take in that heaving chest, the heartbeat speeding up with adrenaline, the soap-scent of his crotch. I would have preferred him unwashed when I took him. I like to carry a man's dense musk in my beard after we part.

Our eyes lock. I continue to dig. Sensing an intrusion he's never encountered before, he shakes his head again and again, trying to dislodge me. Big man, big will. It's like arm-wrestling. But he's only had forty-some years to gather his strength. I've had centuries.

"Put down the gun, Tobias," I say quietly. "I know you're an avid gun-toter, but those days are over. Put down the gun."

He shakes his head. His big hand begins a fine trembling.

It's intoxicating when they fight me. It makes overpowering

them all the more thrilling. Forcing strength and beauty to submit: that's a quest worth the dedication of many lifetimes.

I rummage through his brain, trying to find it, the place from which to rule. Rare is the human whose will I can't subdue. Like wrapping my hand around an uncut diamond, like holding a man's heart-lump in my grasp and squeezing ever so tenderly. The fulcrum with which Archimedes suggested we might move the world.

Here. Here, I think. I press down. Tobias blinks, staggers back, lowering the gun.

"Why don't you put down that gun and fetch me a scotch?" I'm stroking my beard, smiling at this latest in several centuries of triumphs. And, just when I think my fingers have sunk deep enough to encircle, enslave, his will flexes—an abrupt expansion, a hardening, like the sudden strain of an athlete's biceps. His eyes grow wide, and to my amazement, he shakes me off. He raises the gun, pointing it at my face.

"You tell me who the hell you are, you bastard, and what you want, or I'll blow your head off."

"So you're one of those," I say, sitting up. "You really are remarkable. In all these years, I've met only a handful of men who could do what you just did. Warriors and heroes, every one of them. A magnificent will to match a magnificent body."

"Get the fuck out of my bed, asshole." Tobias waves the gun. "And do it slow, or I'll shoot."

"Yes," I say. "Gladly." I obey. I stand in front of him naked, a mere yard's distance between us.

"What the hell?" Tobias stares down at my erection.

"This is what beauty inspires," I say. "Your fault entirely."

"What are you? Some kind of fucking—?"

That's all he gets out before I leap. I'm on him before he can lift his eyes or draw another breath. In a split second, his grip's broken, his gun's on the carpet at his feet and my hands are wrapped around the pulsing trunk of his neck.

"How—?" he gasps, before I dig my thumbs into the flesh over his windpipe and cut off his breath. His big hands claw at mine. His robe falls open as we sway and circle. "Jesus," he croaks. His eyes bulge and water. His face reddens. He's very, very strong; even robbed of air, he weakens very slowly. It takes more time and effort than I ever would have expected to force him backward, step by straining step, to the bed's edge, to force him down and then back onto the sheets.

"And I was trying to make this meeting as cordial as possible," I say, lying on top of him, his nakedness so warm beneath mine, so moist with terror's sweat. "But of course you're a fighter. I should have known you'd opt for troublesome."

All that blood, pounding in his neck as he bucks beneath me. "You're only making me harder," I say, wrapping my legs around his to subdue his panicked kicks. He's been too proud to try to summon aid, but finally now his fear overcomes that pride. Too late, too little breath left. His cries for help are no more than frantic wheezes. I gaze into his eyes, studying the rapid flickering of his long lashes as he pries futilely at my fingers.

"Please," he says, such a small whisper from such a large man.

"We're not done yet," I say. I kiss his full lips, lightly, then strike his temple with my right knuckles—one sharp rap to the skull, as if his head were a door. He grunts. His blue eyes close. Beneath me, he goes limp.

I leave him there, slumped across the bed. For a few minutes I stand by the door, listening. Silence in the hall, no one roused by the brief struggle. Fetching his abandoned scotch, I stand by the window, watching the snow sifting down outside. When I'm certain there will be no interruptions, I light a candle, place it on a side table, and search among his belongings for what's needed next.

Tobias is ready now. Many hours yet till dawn, so I can take my time, I can savor the scotch, stretch out in this big bed beside him, relish the sight of him sprawled unconscious on his back— hairy, handsome and entirely helpless. He's naked now in the candlelight, sleeping his next-to-last sleep. I tousle his blond curls, rub his bearded chin, run a hand over his broad breast. Such a splendor; such an evil. Such a pity that I must erase one in order to erase the other.

With the terry-cloth belt of his robe, I've tied his big wrists together in the small of his back. Not snug-tight, the way I like to rope up my sweet lover Matt, but hurtful-tight. Tobias's politics require it. With a leather belt found in his suitcase, I've bound his arms behind him so tightly his elbows almost touch; I want his big muscles contorted, his joints racked. With another leather belt I've cinched his ankles together. To stop his speech, I've tied two dirty white gym socks together at the toes, stuffed his mouth with the fat, foot-sour knot and secured the ends behind his head. He's exceptionally beautiful this way. The world will be less one loveliness tomorrow.

Tobias shifts beside me, coming awake. Bending over him, I lap his chin. His eyes flicker open, blurry blue. He groans, rolling onto his side. His eyes wander, fall on me, focus. He grits his teeth around the gag, growls deep in his throat and tries to rise. He fails. His muscles strain. Awareness of his thoroughly powerless position fills his eyes. Truly delicious, such frantic surprise. The trammeled thrashing and stifled shouting begin.

"Keep still, Tobias. You'll hurt yourself," I say, but it's too late. Wide as the bed is, his struggles are so violent that he rolls off the edge, landing on the floor with a thump and a grunt.

I slip off the bed to fetch him. He lies stunned, on his side, knees drawn up in a fetal curl, fists clenched against the small of his back. When his struggles recommence, as do his muffled shouts, I stand astride him, then lift a foot and press it hard against the side of his face.

"Be quiet and keep still, or I'll crush your skull."

He obeys immediately.

"You're going to do what you're told?"

Tobias hesitates a second, then nods. How it must pain him, that reluctant recognition of superior strength.

"Good boy." I bend, heaving him upright. He sways on bound feet, glaring at me, panting into the cloth stuffing his mouth, then loses his balance and topples into my arms. I catch him, lifting him beneath shoulders and knees. He stiffens with shock as I carry him to the window.

"Look. It's still snowing," I say, gazing out into the restless sheets of white, then down at him, folded up in my arms as if he were my son. I smile. "You're wondering how a man so much smaller can pick you up?"

He sucks in air through his nose and nods. Shudders course through him.

"I have a secret," I say, "and some stories to tell."

I carry my captive to the bed, gently lower him onto it, and slip onto the sheets beside him. I gaze down at him, at that well-muscled bulk trussed up tight and panting in candlelight. He stares up at me, eyes moist with terror. I love it when they want to sob but their masculine sense of shame won't allow them. Their eyes grow wet at the edges like a farm pond's ice giving way with spring thaw.

"Take a look at you now," I say, dragging a finger over the delicate pink flesh of his gagged lips. "The Virginia senator has nothing to say?"

Tobias shakes his head slowly. How badly he wants to look away or close his eyes, but he can't. Never in all his most agonizing nightmares could he have imagined himself so power-less.

His shuddering is even more violent now that we're in bed together. Plus the building's old, the room's drafty, snow's swarming the windowpanes.

"Are you cold?"

Tobias nods. "Poor boy," I sigh. Stretching out on my back beside him, I pull the covers over us, lean back on the pillows heaped against the headboard and say, "Put your head on my chest." Bound as tightly as he is, it takes a little squirming on his part, a little nudging on mine, till the weight of his big head rests over my heart.

"Isn't this sweet?" I sigh, wrapping an arm around him. "You feel so good against me. Comfortable?"

Tobias shakes his head emphatically. Behind the sock-knot a grunted "Huh-uh."

Chuckling, I play with the hair fringing his nipples. He stiffens against me; jagged trembling runs through him.

"You hate this, don't you? My touching you?"

A slow nod. More trembling.

"Good. Would you like to know why I'm here? Other than to do this?" I tug at his belly-hair now, squeeze the thick muscles of his shoulders and arms, the thick meat of his chest. "Other than to pay homage to your considerable might?"

"Ummm mmm," he mumbles into the socks, breathing heavily through his nose. I pull him closer, sip my scotch and stroke his head of golden curls.

"Let me begin with this," I say. Even after these several centuries, I can't keep the sorrow from my voice, stern as I might want to sound tonight. "In 1730, my lover Angus and I were caught making love, attacked by a gang of men like you. Men who thought their God hated us. Angus died. He was stabbed to death. I was saved for another life."

Tobias emits a low, long groan. His shaking grows more violent.

"Do you understand? This is why I am stronger and faster than you could ever be, why my skin is so chilly against you."

Tobias shakes his head. He gives a small sob.

"You're still shivering. Are you still cold? I am as well. Here, let me hold you closer." Rolling him onto his side, I curl up against him, his broad back to my chest. My left arm pillows his head, my right arm I wrap around him.

"Better. Ah, you're so, so warm," I say, caressing his beefy chest beneath the blanket. "Tobias, do you remember that hateful amendment you helped pass? The one outlawing same-sex marriages in Virginia? The one insuring that 'any contracts between same-sex couples that might approximate marriage would be illegal'? I think that was the wording. Tonight really began there. And with three people with whose fates I'm familiar. I wish you could have known them. Perhaps then you and I would never have met."

I rest my palm against his breastbone. His heart drums madly beneath my hand. I nuzzle his nape, smell the blood coursing beneath his thin, fragile skin and lick my lips.

"There was Charlotte, a bar-buddy of my lover Matt's. She was driving home one night when a drunk driver hit her head-on. Her lover Grace was barred from her hospital room. Thanks to your amendment, Grace was not considered family. So Charlotte died alone. Can you imagine that?"

Another choked sob. A gag-muffled, "No," a shaking of the head.

"Then there was Karen, Matt's friend from college years ago.

Her ex-husband swore to identify her as a lesbian in court if she fought him for custody of their two sons. She hanged herself in her barn. That's the kind of world your laws help create, Tobias. Can you see that?"

"No, no." Muffled, but louder.

"And sweet little Chet, Matt's cousin. Just sixteen years old. Thanks to your adept political maneuvering and all your fundamentalist friends, his high school wouldn't allow a gay-straight alliance. No sympathy from his parents, who told him he was a damned-to-hell monster. The boy drowned himself in Peak Creek last week. My lover's been weeping on and off ever since."

As I whisper in Tobias's ear, I press my hand over his brow, and inside his skull I cause them to appear, the consequences of his demagogic bluster: the bloated body hung off creaking rafters, the pale limbs splayed in gray water, the woman sobbing in a hospital waiting room. Beneath my palm, the images cascade through his brain, on and on, on and on, the pain, the deaths, the fear he's helped create.

Enough. I lift my hand from his forehead, and the stream of stories stops. "They were my kin. Now do you see why I'm here?"

This time a nod. This time a sock-muted "Yes." This time an unchecked stream of silent tears I wipe from his cheeks with my thumb.

"Good." For a full minute I stroke his streaming cheeks, tasting the salt, the remorse, the appetizer of brine. Suddenly, roughly, I roll him onto his belly, climb on top of him and clamp one hand over his gagged mouth.

"What a Christian," I say, stroking the fuzzy crevice between his buttocks. Tobias gasps beneath my grip; his broad shoulders heave.

"Here's your salvation," I say, spitting into my palm then

moistening us both. "Here's your forgiveness." I burrow a wet fingertip into him, and his muscles spasm against me. Manly beauty has always inspired in me an urge to possess, dominate, punish and control. But the combination of beauty and hatefulness that Tobias embodies sparks in me a sadism no human can long survive.

Were I to give him the benefit of the doubt, I might assume that these sobs wracking him are born of guilt in the face of the destruction I've shown him, the misery he's helped create. I suspect, however, that what's really evoking his tears is the certainty of what's about to come, as well as the bodily pain I'm causing as I roughly push one finger in. Men I respect, men like my lover Matt, I take slowly, solicitously. Tobias, well, I'm using very little spit and very little patience.

"Sweet country boy, sweet virile Virginia virgin. You're so tight and sweet and soft inside," I sigh, wedging a wet second finger in. He jerks and whines. Sobs shake him like winter rattling the windowpane.

"If you were fat and old and homely, like most of your right-wing colleagues, you'd be spared this," I say, pulling out my fingers only to nudge my moistened cock against his tightness. "This is what comes of being so proud and handsome," I say, pushing into him an inch.

Now he goes wild beneath me, screaming against my hand, tugging on his bonds, thrashing and bucking. I love such resistance. It only highlights my own supernatural strength. Wrapping an arm around his torso, I let him flail and shout for a minute or two before shoving my cock's entire length into him and simultaneously burying my fangs in his sweaty neck.

I pump into Tobias, Tobias's blood pumps into me: contrapuntal rhythm. Ass full, mouth full. Spilling not a drop, I gulp down his strength, his will, his youth, his manhood; my gray hair, beard and chest pelt slowly blacken in answer. Beneath my hand, he keeps screaming for a while. Beneath my weight, he keeps thrashing for a while. Then, as the tide of his blood recedes, the screams slow, dwindling to barely audible pleas, and the struggles slacken.

Practice allows me perfect timing: I retract my fangs just before he passes out but well after he's too weak to put up any further fight. He simply lies there now, wheezing beneath me with each cock-thrust, bound hands fumbling at nothing, brushing my belly hair as I ride him hard. Occasionally, in response to a particularly savage slamming, he manages a muffled groan. This is a judicial ecstasy I've been long yearning for, so, as much as I would enjoy prolonging this, I'm soon done. Wrapping an arm around his throat, I shove into him one last time, shudder, grunt, explode.

I wake with a start. Sated, I've been happily drowsing on top of him. It is, I sense, about four hours before daybreak. The candle has burnt low. Snow still fills the windowpanes with busy, silent static.

I roll off Tobias and lie beside him. His bonds and gag are still in place; he's still breathing, still conscious. Eyelashes fluttering, slowly he shifts his stare from the sheet to my face. In the candlelight, his cheeks gleam with tears. I kiss his gold-brown goatee and his bloodied neck. I press my lips to his big ass, lap the smooth, pale skin there, the red marks my fingernails left, then spread his cheeks and push my tongue inside him to harvest violation's crimson ooze. What might he have been without evangelical poison in him, the Christians' vicious piety?

He's perfectly still as I untie his elbows, hands and feet. When I prop him up into a sitting position, he slumps against me. When I heft him with eldritch ease into my arms, huge man that he is, his head falls against my face, his arms bounce loosely.

"It's time to end this, Tobias," I whisper. Around the knot of the sock-gag, he takes a deep breath. Exhaling slowly, he nods acquiescence against my beard.

The bathroom is even colder than the bedroom. It's spacious, with a marble sink covered with the tentacles of potted plants, a window of glass bricks against which the thickening snow bats. The shower is simply a tiled corner without a curtain, with a big floor-drain down which I might later rinse any scarlet stains my hunger misses. Carefully I shift docile Tobias from my arms to the floor, turn the water on, adjust its temperature then drag him into the streaming wet warmth. On the floor I sit cross-legged with him in my arms, his heavy linebacker's body cradled in my lap. I nuzzle his gagged mouth, then loosen the socks, let the silencing circle of knotted cloth fall around his neck, and kiss him tenderly on the lips. I caress his rapidly moistening curls, his nipples, his fading heartbeat. His head sags against my shoulder. He hasn't strength enough to groan.

Warm water sluices through my shaggy dark hair, running through my beard to drip over his face. It runs down his thick torso, his hairy belly and mats up his pubes. I cup his flaccid cock in my hand. "Warm enough?"

His lips move silently. Another long draught and he'll be done.

"I'm Derek Maclaine," I say, apropos of nothing.

"You are so beautiful," I sigh, rocking him in my arms. "You were so strong. You could have been so good, so true. Why did you listen to them? What a warrior you could have made. What a brother-in-arms. I would have been proud to love you."

Lifting his limp right hand from the tiles, I hold it in mine. When I squeeze it, with what life he has left he returns the pressure.

I gaze down into Tobias's glazed blue eyes for a long time. "It's all right," I say, smoothing curls off his brow. "Sweet boy."

He smiles up at me sleepily. He lifts his free hand to touch the barbed wire inked into my upper arm, then, with a visible effort, reaches up to brush my tangled black hair and beard before his fingers droop and his hand drops exhausted into his lap.

"Here You are," he whispers in disbelief, words so weak even I can barely discern them. "It's You. You. Oh, Lord, oh, Jesus, I been waiting for You."

Together we listen to the snow-wind beyond the walls, holding hands in the steamy rush of the shower. Prisoners of necessity, we are both late for different destinations, and it is nearly dawn, nearly time to part, but let us sit here for a while yet, pressed together in this warm womb hemmed in by winter. I will stay with Tobias till he closes his eyes, till his hand releases mine, till, soon, soon, he needs me no longer.

THE BOY IN SUMMER

Shaun Levin

1. The Boy Discovers Playgirl

There was a copy in his parents' bedroom on the bottom shelf of their cupboard by the bed, hidden under a pile of *Penthouse* magazines. Burt Reynolds was the centerfold, or someone like him. Charles Bronson, perhaps. That kind of look: dark, mustached, hairy chested. Suave is a word that comes to mind. The Boy felt—it was like touching—that he'd never been so close to the naked body of a man and been able to stroke it. He was sixteen. It was the first reciprocal experience of his adult life. He was, literally, giddy with desire. He rushed downstairs to the bathroom, locked the door, sat on the toilet and masturbated until he came. Then he did it again.

It was the summer holidays. Long lazy days of profound heat, moving between all-morning television and hours on the beach. The Boy's parents were at work. Later that afternoon, there'd be time for The Boy to masturbate again before they got home for dinner. That evening there was blood in his urine; it was dark, and The Boy was convinced this was further evidence of his gradual transformation into a girl. His nipples ached and were growing bigger. Now he was having his first period.

That summer The Boy sunbathed naked on the lawn in the back garden of their new home. He took his towel and walked in his underwear from the patio into the middle of the grass, then lay on his back, stripped and covered his genitals with his briefs. The Boy believed that if he closed his eyes he would not be seen. He lay there naked, soaking up the sun as if it had the power to transport him, his skin turning brown in the middle of the week in the middle of the day in the middle of the lawn in the middle of a cluster of houses, newly built, The Boy exposed like a sacrifice for all to see.

The Boy was in love with a boy at his school, an agricultural school outside the town they lived in, a boy called A who boarded there, a boy who, The Boy now thinks, was in love with him, too, but, he wants to say, in a different way. Though maybe it wasn't different. The Boy wanted to be as slender and muscled as A, as charming and as confident, as loved. As unafraid. The Boy bought gifts for A: bars of soap in particular and shampoo. A's hair was long and brown and curly. Much like The Boy's was when he stood in that car park by the beach with his arms across his chest, A holding the camera and saying *Smile*.

2. *The Boy on the Beach*

The Boy is seventeen when it happens for the first time, and by the first time he means his first time as an adult, because there were times when it happened when The Boy was a boy, and by a boy he means a boy of nine or ten. Maybe a bit older, but no more than thirteen. Fourteen at the most.

The Boy is bronzed. He has been coming here all summer and the man has seen him, but this is the first time the man has stopped his jeep and parked close enough to see every detail of The Boy's body. The Boy steps out of the sea and walks toward his towel on the sand at the edge of the low dunes by the scrub that grows on the stretch between the beach and the gravel road. The Boy is naked and slim and tall with a long neck. He walks slowly; he knows he is being watched by the man who sits in his jeep with his penis in his hand. Hair grows between The Boy's nipples, such beautiful soft breasts, and although the man prefers the flat-chested boys, he cannot take his eyes off The Boy, his gentle mound of pubic hair, the curve of his hips, the slimness of his arms, the way the sun reflects off his wet shoulders, his curls, bleached blond by the sun. The Boy lies on his stomach, turns his head to the side and looks directly at the man. The man doesn't know what to do with this lust that is excessive and inescapable.

The man comes over to The Boy. He is not the first man to talk to him, but The Boy is as excited and as terrified as if he were. The Boy will come to recognize this feeling of exhilarated panic—it won't go away—this feeling of imminent death; an excitement and terror so profound it threatens to annihilate him. The man asks The Boy to turn over. It's what The Boy has been waiting for, rehearsed when he was ten and again at fourteen; now he is choosing this kind of touch. This is who The Boy will be for the rest of his life.

Every time The Boy goes back to the beach after this day he will wait for the man to appear, the man who will take him for rides in his jeep and park farther up the coast and swim with him, and then just that once, the last time they meet, the man will kneel before The Boy and ask to be penetrated. He will expose his older-man's smooth brown arsehole and lower himself onto The Boy's penis and pleasure himself again and again and again.

The beach stretches for miles. The sea is a lesson in moderation. The Boy reenters the sea to wash traces of the man's feces off his penis, and by the time he has swum back to the shore and walked back to his towel, the man has gone. When The Boy sees the man in town, the man ignores him, perhaps because The Boy is the same age as the man's son.

3. *The Boy and His Daddy*

If The Boy was a dog his Daddy would let him eat out of the palm of his hand and lick between his fingers.

If The Boy was a dog his Daddy would take him for runs on the beach after work in the evenings, to the harbor wall and back, and when his Daddy dashed into the water for a quick dip The Boy would bark at the waves and roll in the sand and work himself up into such a frenzy that when his Daddy came out of the water The Boy would run to him and jump on his chest and make his Daddy laugh and his Daddy would say: *Good boy.*

If The Boy was a dog he wouldn't be scared of his Daddy because he'd know his Daddy loved him. Even when his Daddy said, *Silly boy*, The Boy would hear *I love you*, and when his Daddy smacked The Boy's nose or rubbed it in his own urine, The Boy would know there was no one in the world who loved him as much as his Daddy.

If The Boy was a dog his unwashed fur would smell of sweat and grass and shit and his Daddy would say *Shit, boy, you stink,* and he'd scratch the folds of flesh under The Boy's chin and smile at him and say: *Good dog.*

If The Boy was a dog his Daddy would lift him into the bath and spray warm water on him and lather him with special shampoo and dig his fingers into his flesh and knead him and soothe him, and when he was done his Daddy would rinse the soap off The Boy's fur, and The Boy would shake his body and spray water all over his Daddy, and they'd laugh together and The Boy would bark and they'd wrestle on the floor and his Daddy would hold him tight, both arms around him, and The Boy would struggle and run away because that's what he does when he is overwhelmed with joy.

If The Boy was a dog he would sleep in the kitchen or in the backyard in a basket padded with his Daddy's old blankets and he'd go round and round until he found the perfect position, and he'd lie there with his head peering over the rim of the basket and wait for his Daddy and everybody else in the house to get into bed and turn off the lights, and only then would The Boy close his eyes.

If The Boy was a dog he would dream of long beaches and crashing waves and the moon and thieves. He would dream of vast stretches of lawn and beds of hydrangeas in whose shade he would sleep on hot days. The Boy would dream of raw flesh and dog biscuits and the thrill of begging for leftovers and the strength of the hand that feeds him.

4. *The Boy in the Mountains*

The Boy goes to the baths to be adored, to meet a young man like the man a few days ago who leaned in closer to him as The Boy got up to walk away (he'd had enough). The man cupped The Boy's breasts in his palms and knelt before him to suck on his penis, gulp on it, make those gulping noises—and even when The Boy had gone soft and insisted the young man suck someone else's, like the cock of the man sitting next to him, a cock much harder and bigger than his, the young man obliged only momentarily, to obey, not for his own pleasure. Then the young man returned to The Boy's penis. To gulp it down. And when The Boy had made to leave, the young man leaned in closer and said: *Please*. As in: *Please don't go*. As in: *Please stay*. As in: *Please*.

The Boy is rarely asked to stay. And even when he does stay, he is not the kind of person to stay for very long.

Abandonment is in his genes. His great-grandfather left a family of ten and went to spend his last days in Palestine; The Boy's grandmother was handed over to childless neighbors to bring up as their own; The Boy's father was sent to live with cousins while *his* father went on drunken binges and his mother left to live with her sisters; The Boy has an estranged sibling in Africa; he has several ex-boyfriends whom he left long before he should have.

The Boy grew up in a tribe of aunties and uncles. Every male in the family, every friend of his parents, was *uncle*. Some were dark and wore black Speedos, some were covered in lush hair, some were called playboys and had girlfriends who weren't Jewish. His aunties played bridge and baked cakes to raise money for the Jews in the land of the Jews. The Boy had an uncle who touched him. The Boy might be making this up, misremembering, but that is inevitable when it comes to memory. Sometimes he is sure it happened. At least once, at night, in the mountains or out at sea on a boat or in a pool shed, away from the family, away from everything.

"What a beautiful boy," his uncle had said. (The Boy remembers kissing his uncle, or at least leaning in to kiss him—did the uncle turn his head?—did he say: *I am proud of you*...for what? Catching a fish? Climbing a mountain? But the memory is a blur. The Boy is not sure who said what; all he has is this gesture of leaning in toward the uncle while stepping out of the uncle's car, expecting a kiss. As if to say: *Please*.)

There is a picture of The Boy in his rugby socks taken before the ascent into the mountains. He looks ugly, ugly in the way Jewish women in the Middle Ages made themselves undesirable to the Cossacks by shaving their heads. The Boy's blond hair and the abundance of redheads in his family only prove the futility of such tactics.

5. *The Boy Looks at A*

The Boy and A are tanned and smiling in their white crewneck T-shirts. Behind them: solar panels and water tanks and television antennae. A is smiling at the camera (his friend is taking the picture) and The Boy is smiling at A, his expression guarded, the corners of his mouth pulled back, his lips stretched, as if caught in the midst of saying something, or reining in a smile that wants to devour his face. The Boy has a defined jawline and clear skin; his hair is dark and cropped close to the skull. A has short hair, too. Over time it will grow longer, it will be tightly curled (his mother is Yemenite) and A will try various methods to straighten it. He will use a curling iron and will burn his hair.

By looking at A, The Boy must ignore A's friend, the friend who is taking the picture. The Boy does this often, ignores the people he dislikes, turns his head away and *voila!* they're gone. A is the focus of this picture: the viewer's gaze and the gaze of The Boy are on him. The Boy is not sure how he feels about being caught on camera, his love for A so evident and frozen in time. He does not have many pictures of himself as a boy with a boy he loves, both of them looking happy.

In a picture of two there is always a third (unless they're using the self-timer). With two, there is a triangle of gazes, eyes looking at each other: she at us, he at her, me at him. But the picture rarely reveals who is taking it (unless there's a self-timer, but even then we cannot be sure), and we can never know who the photographer is looking at. We can guess, because A is looking into the camera; it's as if The Boy isn't there, as if just A and his friend, that friend who is taking the picture, as if just they are there.

In another picture of The Boy with another man there is a third person, but the third person is absent; she is The Man's wife. The Man's wife knows nothing about The Boy. She knows nothing about The Man and The Boy's goings-on, at least this is what The Man believes, so The Boy plays along. The Boy takes the picture with a timer to have a record of this day. That's what he says to The Man: *I want to remember this day.* The real reason for the picture is that The Man will not be The Boy's lover for much longer. Within a month, The Boy will end it. The Boy is already thinking of the future; he is already there with another lover looking back at this time, at this ex-lover.

6. *A Story about The Boy*

The Boy likes to be reminded of himself. He likes stories told by others about who he was. One story was told to him by an ex-boyfriend who now lives in San Francisco with a man he met on a bus in Nicaragua twenty years ago. This ex-boyfriend told The Boy how proud he used to feel to be his boyfriend.

"Everyone looked at you when we went out," he said. "And I used to think: *He's mine.*"

The Boy was amused when his ex-boyfriend told him this. Amused, though, is not the word to describe how The Boy felt.

Some random memories: Lying on the beach one day, The Boy (not yet eighteen) is approached by a man who invites him to take part in a porn movie. The Boy plays in the waves with a French girl. The Boy goes jogging on the beach late at night with his lover, goes to Prague with his lover and to Barcelona with his lover, and…but all this is in the years to come.

BLOSSOMS IN AUTUMN

Boris Pintar

Translated from the Slovenian by Rawley Grau

Years had passed since Slavko marked his half century. A hard life had rewarded him with excess pounds; the hair on the top of his head had almost entirely disappeared, while the back and sides had turned gray—and not that silvery gray that sometimes even looks fashionable; no, this was a dirty yellowishness, like the color that never quite comes off the fingers of avid smokers. Hair sprouted from his ears, from his nose, from the top of his nose, down his back, across his stomach, everywhere it had never been in his youth; and where the first hair of his puberty had appeared—on his ankles, which he once so proudly compared at phys ed with the ankles of his schoolmates—the skin was now bare, with only faint dots left as on a plucked hen to tell of his once-mighty bristles. The doctor had said he had an above-average supply of the male hormone that governed his transformation. He lived alone. His friends—those he hadn't fallen out with—had gradually died off or grown distant. The more time he spent by himself, the more his desire grew for the warmth of another body, and the older he got, the younger were the men who caught his eye. *Where is the crossing point?* he sometimes asked himself in dread, for he saw no sign of a more tranquil old age, of enjoying a life of contented domesticity dishing the dirt with the people he knew.

The call of his urges grew louder and louder; he got excited just by looking out the window of his apartment at the school-yard across the street and the teenage boys chasing the ball. An inner voice was constantly compelling him to go out and meet new people and would send him into a funk if he failed to get them into bed. It was always somebody new, always younger and younger—he had no time for old acquaintances, who phoned him less and less often. He was wealthy enough to hire hand-some young men to come to his house to satisfy his desires, and he had done so a number of times, but still he longed for love. The men to whom he openly paid the agreed price kept a certain distance from him, as if he repulsed them. They expressed them-selves mechanically; they might as well have been stuffing jelly doughnuts in a pastry shop: *What do you like to do? What do you want me to do to you? Turn over! Did you come? Okay, see ya!* They never opened their mouths wide enough for him to stick his tongue in; it was as if he was diseased—*Please, don't get personal!*—they never kissed him, never stroked him, never tried to get him aroused; never caressed him, hugged him, beat him; he was the one who always had to climb on top of them, tongue them front and back, turn them over, as if *they* were paying *him*. They didn't even want to touch him—all to preserve that disinterested pose, so they could say they weren't queer but only did it for the money. *Tell me what you want; you give me head, I fuck you; I don't get fucked, I don't give head, sorry, chum!—*

But who's paying here?—*You knew the score, take it or leave it!*—and what choice did he have when his urges got stronger every year? He longed to have someone want him, at least a little, even if not for real; to have someone prove to him that even *he* had something to offer a man, more than just drugs and money; he longed for them all not to be so direct, so hurried, so impersonal; he longed to have someone play the game of seduction with him, to sleep next to a warm body, to wake up in the same bed with someone and have breakfast together after morning sex. This was why he still went out to the clubs where he'd meet young people—from the clubs on skyscraper terraces, which at night offered a New York–like view of castle turrets and church belfries, to the ones so deep below ground it seemed there was nowhere for the sewage to drain so it just accumulated right there. His age and the way he looked made him stand out among the young bodies in tight-fitting pants and shimmering Lycra T-shirts that clearly displayed the separate body parts, still in their recognizable shapes—which he could no longer say of himself when he looked in the mirror. He dressed as youthfully as he could, hiding a few pounds with certain fashion tricks, and armed himself with drugs, his ticket into the world of the young. He knew dealers; he knew chemists who manufactured Ecstasy in home laboratories; and he had mastered in every nuance the street talk of youth, which left him sounding ridiculous whenever he forgot himself around older folks.

There was a puddle of water and urine on the floor that had overflowed from a clogged urinal, and although its ocher was now diluted, the acrid reek in the nostrils testified to its many years' presence in this poorly lit room of broken, graffiti-scrawled white tile. The folk art on the walls portrayed queer fantasies come to life: ever-bigger cocks in ever-greater numbers—up the ass, in the mouth, inside the head. The cold draft that entered through a vent beneath the ceiling could not expel the odor of piss that penetrated every pore. Slavko was aware of neither the cold nor the stench; he had taken some X and had a few gin-and-colas, which made him feel both high and tranquil and certainly bolder and braver, his dick rock hard whenever he brushed up against some teenager on the dance floor. Younger guys couldn't get it up when they took X, but it had precisely the opposite effect on him. But first he had to take a leak. He opened his zipper, pulled out his whizzer and let loose a pressurized pale stream in all directions, including down his pants, until he managed to tug the foreskin back and aim at the urinal, which was getting dangerously full and threatening to overflow. He glanced around at the other urinals and on his left noticed a boy whose pee-flow had just ended. Slavko instantly averted his eyes, but then, remembering that he was more courageous now, unabashedly looked back down at the boy's dick, which he was still shaking dry—and now stroking it, making it thicker—and Slavko thought it could be a rather good-sized morsel if only he had the chance to work it over with his mouth. He glanced up at the face of the guy, who was looking straight into his eyes, which he instantly redirected back toward the guy's cock. He knew he should say something but couldn't think what.

"Want some X, dude?"

"You got some?"

Slavko reached into the pocket of his jeans and pulled out a plastic bag of tiny pills; then, with his dick still hanging out of his pants, he took a pill from the bag and placed it in the mouth of the boy, who swallowed it dry as he kept stroking his cock. Slavko, who now felt no fear at all about staring at the boy's rod, stretched out his hand and grasped this warm rising loaf, which smelled of mama's kitchen.

"You like it, huh?"

"May I?" Slavko said, bending over, about to kneel in the cold puddle of water and piss.

"A cock like this you got to pay for!"

"Just a little, please!"

"It's fifty or nothing. I need the money for drinks and my mobile."

"Okay, but only if you come to my place. I'm not paying fifty euros to suck some guy off in the john!" said Slavko, sobering up and switching from seduction to business mode.

"So you want me to do you? You live far from here?"

"A couple of blocks. I've got my car outside."

Slavko needed some time to get himself into the low seat of his Porsche but then took off so fast the wide tires squealed as he turned onto the road. He ran through a few yellow lights to show off the Porsche's acceleration to his new partner, and in no time at all they were in front of his house in a quiet residential neighborhood in the middle of the city. He opened the garage door with a remote and led his guest up some inside stairs into a luxurious living room filled with Versace furniture, which evoked a golden-age happiness for the twenty-first century.

"Would you like a drink? Just put your coat anywhere! What's your name, by the way?"

"Sebastijan."

The boy removed his leather cap, and his thick, wavy, raven hair, shimmering like the metallic color of the Porsche, tumbled over his ears, though it kept the forehead-to-nape flow a strong hair gel had set in place. The haircut recalled the era of *A Streetcar Named Desire* and the young Marlon Brando, whose photo adorned Slavko's bathroom.

"Whiskey if you got it."

"Sure do."

Only now did Slavko notice the full beauty of Sebastijan's symmetrical face; the smooth, white, poreless skin; the straight nose, the full lips, the slightly dimpled cheeks free of the age creases that run from nose to chin—which he himself had had smoothed away with plastic surgery—the thick black eyebrows beneath a high, even forehead; the curved black eyelashes, as long as a woman's; and the dark pupils set in the white sclera of his eyes. Sebastijan took off his tight, black leather motorcycle jacket, padded at the elbows and shoulders and under it wore a sleeveless T-shirt, which hung on him as loosely as his jeans did—but this hardly kept Slavko from imagining every muscle beneath the clothes. The boy looked firm to him, not too muscular but just enough so it was impossible to detect the least bit of fat on his body; he was of medium height and well proportioned, and Slavko felt as though he could cook, wash, iron and clean for this boy for the rest of his life.

"So you into sports?"

"Martial arts. You know anything about it? I'm a European and national champion. I still work out now, just for myself. And I know how to party."

"Want to do a line?"

He would give anything to make the encounter last longer. From a drawer that held his table linen he extracted a plastic bag with white powder and handed it trustingly to Sebastijan, even though it contained enough to last the whole month. Sebastijan, spreading his legs in a manly way, sat down on the white sofa in front of the coffee table, which had an inlaid sun on its marble top and fluted legs, and shook a little of the white powder onto the table's smooth surface, took a plastic card from the back pocket of his jeans and started crushing the cocaine with its edge. Slavko brought over an unopened bottle of twenty-five-year-old Chivas Regal—which was so expensive he might have been saving it for his wedding—two glasses and a pitcher of ice with tongs, then sat down on the sofa, more than half of which was taken up by Sebastijan, and crossed his legs. In his hand he held a rolled-up fifty-euro bill, which Sebastijan would get, after they were done with it, as a piece of discarded paraphernalia and not as payment for a love that was so sincere no amount of money could express its worth. With the plastic card Sebastijan divided the powder on the marble into two lines. Slavko stuck one end of the rolled-up banknote into a nostril, bent over the table and vacuumed up a line with the other end. Then leaning back, he inhaled deeply, let out a grunt from the pleasure and the burn and gave the little tube to Sebastijan, who vacuumed up the second line and leaned back on the sofa without making any sound at all of either pleasure or displeasure.

For Slavko, getting high was the foreplay, and he now set to work unbuttoning Sebastijan's jeans in search of the source of life. Sebastijan did not resist. He took the expensive whiskey from the table, undid the sealed cork and drank it straight out of the bottle, without ice. Slavko, meanwhile, freed Sebastijan's cock—of considerable size even in a flaccid state—and his heavy balls. The area around the boy's cock was clean shaven; so, too, were the balls and, as Slavko could feel with his hand, his ass. He took hold of the thick dick, put it in his mouth and tried every technique he knew—with tongue, teeth, lips and throat—to get it to stand up. Slowly it started getting bigger—he wasn't totally out of condition yet—and he took it deeper into his mouth, could feel it in his throat; though nearly gagging, he didn't stop; he wanted to see it in its fullness. When the cock was hard enough to stand on its own, he took it out of his mouth and examined it close up, like a work of art he longed to touch but was afraid of triggering an alarm. It was straight, over eight inches long, thick, evenly proportioned with a rounded pink head, which the foreskin had slipped down from, and a prominent vein that curved along it like ivy; the circumference, too, had to be close to eight inches—he had developed a mastery of dimensions ever since he once ordered over the Internet a latex cast of a porn star's actual cock, which had come with all the vital statistics— but *this* cock was even lovelier, shapelier, and most of all, warmer and livelier, and unlike Kris's, which he kept in his dresser, it possessed an expressive desire. He desired to feel its desire inside himself and started undressing. When he undid his vest, his belly drooped down over his belt. He was covered in front by a dense mat of black, gray and yellow hair, which made it impossible to tell where his chest ended and his abdomen began; his dick was hidden deep beneath his belly and his buttocks blended with his thick legs in a vast blob, across which oily mounds rose like volcanoes, some now extinct and plugged with scab. Naked as from his mother's loins, only with a lot more hair and padding, he knelt on the floor, raised his bum in the air and placed his head between Sebastijan's legs, so as to stiffen desire with his tongue in ultimate yearning.

When it seemed to him that Sebastijan's dick was hard enough, Slavko gestured with his hand that now he would take it in his ass, and the boy lifted himself up lethargically, tugged his jeans down to the knees, so it was possible to see his muscular thighs with their sparse short black hairs and then knelt behind him and spread his legs apart, legs now hairless below the knees and adorned with blue veins, like the grooves on an ancient column that had collapsed under too much weight. Slavko inhaled some poppers from a little bottle, first in one nostril, then in the other, and felt he was as open as a book capable of receiving in itself all that was holy in this world. Sebastijan knelt behind this furry mass, which quivered like meat jelly, and the sharp bristles tingled the sensitive glans as he stuck his penis in the chasm between Slavko's thighs. Slavko knew he'd have to help the boy find his way and spread open his rippling asscheeks with his hands, so that Sebastijan saw Slavko's cabbagey hole staring up at him, overgrown with matted hair and edged on one side by gnarled veins, like pork cracklings growing on a pig's butt, and on the other by scabbing from hemorrhoids wounded in his most recent shit. Sebastijan leaned on Slavko's back with his hands, looked up at the ceiling and took aim. Slavko let out a sneeze, blood trickled from his nose, and Sebastijan, glancing down at his cock, which had gone limp before it could penetrate anything, saw that it was smeared with blood.

"You didn't crush the coke enough! And you're not at all hard. Give me a sec, I'll be right back!"

When he returned from the bathroom, having wiped his nose and ass, Slavko handed a Viagra pill to Sebastijan, who downed it with whiskey; he didn't need one himself. The Viagra would be working in about half an hour, if the boy got even a little aroused, so Slavko started piling on the tenderness. He stripped him naked and was astounded by the boy's firm and well-proportioned body; although he was used to young guys, he had never felt toward anyone an attraction of this magnitude. He laid Sebastijan on his back and applied all his arts: a combination of erotic massage, acupuncture, chiropractic and other spiritualities he had learned from self-help books. Every muscle on the boy's abdomen was perfectly formed; his clean-shaven pectorals were still well defined, and Slavko bit one of the nipples a little too hard on purpose just to hear his voice, for he was lying beneath him as if dead. A full-body tongue massage can reveal new erogenous zones, and straight guys get turned on when you lick their asses, so Slavko lifted up Sebastijan's legs—the boy was so flexible he could have done a full split in the air—and moved his tongue closer to the solid, clean-shaven pink butt, which might have broken his nose had the boy clenched it. The anus, so tightly shut it was barely visible, had a slightly sweet taste from the Chanel Allure Sport cologne the boy had scented it with, since geezers were always trying to stick their tongues up there. By tongue-massaging the sphincter, Slavko got Sebastijan's dick to stand up again; then he squatted over him as if to sit on him—but when he spread his asscheeks with his hands so the boy could enter, the inflatable dragon instantly deflated. He saw that it wasn't going to work and got himself ready to fuck Sebastijan instead, since his own dick was still so hard it hurt. Raising Sebastijan's martial-arts legs, he brought his crooked hard-on right up to the boy's blossom so as to penetrate that open-sesame cave. He aimed his dick, solid as a rock, right at the navel of the world, but he couldn't get it in, even though it was a lot smaller than Sebastijan's.

"Have some poppers; it'll make it easier!" He held the little bottle up to one of Sebastijan's nostrils and closed the other with his hand. And when the boy had inhaled the fumes of the liquid, which smelled like glue, he repeated the procedure with the second nostril. Then he lifted Sebastijan's ass a little off the floor and got his dick's pointy knob to go inside, but Sebastijan pushed it out with a yelp.

"Have some more poppers and it won't hurt! Here, take a big whiff!"

Sebastijan was pale, sweat beading on his forehead. He took a deep whiff of the poppers, a few times in each nostril, and seemed to be lying there completely open, when all at once his body tightened in a convulsion; he gripped his chest and looked straight at Slavko with wide-open eyes. Slavko was terrified for a moment, but then he lay down next to the boy and started caressing him, warming him with the heat of his own ample body.

* * *

When he woke up in the morning, Sebastijan was still lying next to him, his open lips proffering an intimate kiss, his cock hard if no longer warm—and now it did not go limp at the sight of Slavko's withered blossom but satisfied him to the full. After a shared breakfast, Slavko went out and bought the biggest freezer he could find.

AND HIS BROTHER CAME TOO

Tony Pike

The following events took place in the English university city of Oxford, nearly thirty years ago: a time when no gay guy needed to sheathe himself in rubber when he fucked his fellow men. According to the law of the time all individuals involved should have been twenty-one or more. In fact they were all eighteen or less....

If David had told Gary that he fucked his own little brother, Gary would have been surprised as well as titillated. But what he actually told him, beginning in the bar of the White Horse and ending up sitting on the bank of the River Cherwell in the autumn dusk, surprised and titillated him even more. David's little brother Mark, now sixteen, actually fucked David, or had done when he was younger, though they hadn't done it in the last year or so. By the time David had told Gary how this had come about (which, unfortunately, there isn't space to detail here), they were both mightily excited and were obliged to unzip each other where they sat and give their substantial cocks relief with crossed hands. Inevitably they both spunked heavily over their jeans and were glad of the oncoming darkness when they walked back to college, saying hallo in the streets to other students whom they knew but who—with luck—would not notice in the gloom the still wet stains on their denims. They had been spotted on the riverbank, however, by the mysterious blond twins, who had walked by on the other side of the water and hailed them with a wave—but they weren't sure what, if anything, the twins had actually seen.

Gary and David had only been at Oxford for a couple of weeks. Both freshmen, aged eighteen, they had clicked at once, fallen for each other, and were now almost as inseparable as the blond twins, especially at bedtime. (The twins' bedtime habits were unknown.) Now back in David's room and getting ready for David's narrow bed, Gary said, "Your brother sounds a character. I'd like to meet him sometime."

"Did I forget to tell you?" David answered. "Mark's got an interview here in two weeks' time; he's hoping for a place next year. He'll be coming up for a couple of nights. You'll get to meet him then."

But before that could happen David left Oxford (and Gary) to spend a weekend at home: it was his father's birthday, and he felt he couldn't not go, since it coincided with a weekend. "You'll have to find someone else to play with while I'm away," he told Gary. "Though I can't immediately imagine who." They had talked a bit about who among their fellow students might be gay or at any rate up for having sex with other boys but had drawn no definite conclusions.

"I'm sure I'll find someone," Gary assured him good humoredly. "You, no doubt, will be having it away with baby brother Mark while you're at home."

"Shouldn't be a bit surprised," David answered with a little smile.

* * *

In the end it was not that Gary found someone, but that someone found Gary. He was sitting alone in the Junior Common Room bar on the Friday evening, when he was joined by a petite and pretty young man with cheeky dark eyes and a mop of thick, black curls. They'd met a few times during Freshers' Week, and Gary remembered that his name was Rob. He had not forgotten that he'd thought him decidedly attractive, before his attention had been so comprehensively distracted by the arrival of David.

The diminutive Rob turned out to have a diminutive cock as well, sweet and dainty, with a tiny foreskin, and it was furnished with a solitary ball, quail's egg sized. It had a habit, Gary discovered, of coming prematurely and unexpectedly, without needing the coaxing of anyone's hand, as soon as Rob got undressed for sex. This distressed and embarrassed the inexperienced Rob at first, but Gary, discovering that Rob was very quickly able to recover himself and shoot a further milky load in more controlled circumstances just minutes later, was able to reassure him and calm his anxieties. All that, Gary said, was just fine. When, on the Saturday, Rob first penetrated Gary with his rapid-reaction little penis, it tickled Gary like a finger-fuck, but it made Gary spout his own spring of sperm pretty quickly all the same. The two of them got on famously and stayed together—mostly in Gary's bed—for the whole weekend.

Rob finally left Gary's room toward the end of Sunday afternoon. "I know you said David won't mind, and that he told you to find someone else for the weekend," Rob said. "But I'm sure he'd prefer not to come back and find that someone actually in your bed. Even if he has been rogering his own brother all weekend. As you tell me he does."

"I told you his brother rogers him." Gary was anxious to set the record straight. "Or used to do. He's never fucked his brother, apparently. Mind you, that was before this weekend. Things may have changed. He'd never fucked anyone before he fucked me at the beginning of term."

Before Rob finally left, Gary told him, "We'll have a return match sometime soon. Maybe David might like to stick his oar in too...metaphorically speaking."

On his return, David wanted to hear all of Gary's adventures—if he'd had any. And Gary regaled him with the story of his weekend and Rob's. David sounded more than a bit interested in future possibilities with Rob, but he glanced rather doubtfully at Gary's single bed. It was cozy enough for two, he thought, but he rather wondered whether it would comfortably accommodate three.

"Rob's very small," Gary reminded him optimistically. "Anyway, what about you?"

A grin spread all the way from David's left ear to his right. "I evened up the score at last," he said. "I fucked my little brother."

In less than a week that famous little brother was in Oxford for his interview. He arrived in the afternoon of the day before, and was promptly shown to one of the spare bedrooms that interview candidates were usually given. (Something that both Gary and David remembered from the year before.) After that he was taken to meet Gary. "You two are so alike!" was the first thing Mark blurted out after they had shaken hands. "David never told me. You might be cousins. Or, if your hair wasn't different colors, almost twins."

Gary, in his turn, was as surprised by Mark's appearance as Mark had been by his. Where David was a little more than medium height and of a slim if muscular build, Mark was rather short and stocky. But if small, he gave the appearance of being pretty strong. His face was round and open, his eyes blue and wide and friendly. He had a small snub nose. He was wearing the top part of his school uniform: blazer, shirt and a tie, which was loose at the neck. It was a bit of a compromise though. Below, he had on tight blue jeans which neatly hugged his sturdy thighs and calves, and he wore trainers on his feet. He looked like a cross between a real schoolboy and a rent boy whose gambit is to dress like one. More than anything else though, the kid oozed sex appeal from every pore.

"Wow," said Gary, forgetting his manners in his surprise. "You look good, kid. David forgot to tell me what a handsome boy you are."

"He failed to pass on the same information regarding you," said the boy, "although he told me pretty well everything else. Well, I mean, he left out a few other things, I guess."

Gary forbore to ask what those things might be. Size of dick, perhaps? That he was circumcised? And that when he masturbated, he preferred to do it slowly?

David spoke. "I was wondering if you could look after Mark for me this evening. Be my stand-in and give him a tour of Oxford. Show the kid the inside of a few pubs. Not too many, mind—he does have an interview tomorrow."

Gary found his heart cheering at the prospect of an evening with a cute kid who seemed to have a nice personality, and about whose sexual habits he already knew more than a little. And clearly, Mark had more than an inkling about Gary's own. It promised to be a fun evening. "Sure," he told David. "Of course I'll do that, if Mark would like it too." Mark nodded and grinned. "But what about you? Won't you come with us?"

David looked a bit sheepish for a moment. But only for a moment. "Actually," he said, "I've got something on with your little friend Rob."

"Oh, have you, now?" Gary said archly and saw Mark catch his eye and wink at him. He sniggered in reply but asked no further questions.

Oxford after dark, on an early autumn evening, took on the look it had worn a hundred, two hundred—in places six hundred— years ago. Old-fashioned streetlamps in antique cast-iron frames cast gleaming glances along shadowy streets. Gothic windows peered darkly or with a lemony light. Even the names of the streets that Gary took Mark wandering through seemed to come alive with the ghosts of history: Friars' Entry, Longwall Street, Holywell. Fearsome gargoyles looked down at them from the pediments of the Sheldonian Theatre, and moonlight winked and flittered through the traceried battlements of St. Mary's church. Gary felt oddly proud of his new charge: his lovely friend's very pretty, chunky little brother, two years younger than himself, walking at his side in his very tight blue jeans, the top of his head level with Gary's eyes. And not least of the attractions of this novel situation was the fact that Mark seemed more than ready to steer the conversation, at every opportunity, round to the subject of sex.

They sampled the wares of a number of the city center's pubs: the Bear in Blue Boar Street, the Lamb and Flag in the Broad, the White Horse in the Corn. "I suppose I owe it to you," Mark said to Gary, "that I got fucked by David last time he came home."

"I hope you won't hold that against me," Gary said. They were sitting at the same candlelit table in the alcove in the White Horse where, a few weeks earlier, David had begun to tell Gary about his teenage adventures with Mark.

"Quite the reverse actually," said Mark now. "He'd never fucked anyone before he first did you. Now he's kind of got the bug. Couldn't get enough of it with me." He leaned across the table conspiratorially, his eyes twinkling with mischief. "And I wouldn't be surprised if he's busy ramming his rod into little Rob up in his bedroom even as we speak." He leaned back again. "Anyway, I'm not complaining. I'd never been fucked before. My friends at school mostly wank me, and I them. Which is great. But fucking's kind of extra isn't it?"

Gary blinked—this was all pretty frank from a schoolboy he'd only just met and in a crowded pub—but he had to agree that it was.

"I'm hoping I'll get a fuck from you this evening," Mark went blithely on. "Though maybe that's wishful thinking. First meeting and everything. But at the very least I'm looking forward to seeing your cock. David tells me it's very nice."

"It's very much like his, to be honest," said Gary. "In color, shape and size. Seven and three-quarter inches each. The only major difference is that he's got a foreskin and I haven't. A minor source of regret, that is," Gary admitted. "I'm slightly jealous of his."

"Well, I hope you won't be too jealous of me then," said Mark. "I've got a foreskin too. I'll show you later."

Gary smiled. "I'll look forward to that. And if you're looking forward to getting fucked by me tonight—well, I was a bit surprised to be told that but...after such an invitation, I can hardly refuse. Though maybe your brother won't be too happy about it."

"I already told him that was my ambition for this evening. He told me not to count on it, but he wished me luck all the same." Mark took a swig of lager and then looked around the crowded bar. "It'd be fun to do it right here, wouldn't it?" he said, a mischievous twinkle in his eyes. "In the middle of the floor. In front of all these people. Cheering us on."

Gary laughed. "You're an outrageous boy! Nice idea though,

except the nice people wouldn't be cheering us on; they'd be unceremoniously chucking us out and calling the police. Fantasy is one thing; real life is quite another."

"Pity," said Mark. "Hey, guess what?"

"What now?" said Gary with mock weariness.

"I've just pulled my cock out of my jeans. It's really stiff already."

There was no way Gary could check whether this was true. A heavy oak table lay between them, and he would have had to either stand up and peer over it or get down on his knees on the floor and peer up from underneath. Both moves would have drawn a lot of attention from the other customers in the pub, and attention was the last thing Gary wanted when he was escorting a boy who, according to the law, was too young to be drinking beer in a pub at all. "You're a very naughty boy," he said instead, smiling.

"Dare you to get yours out," Mark said. "Go on."

"It's all very well for you," Gary told him firmly, "snugly hidden behind the table. But I'm sitting in full public view. You can see it later. I promise."

Mark nudged the conversation a little way back the way it had come—though not all that far. "About this fuck then," he said. "So you've vetoed the floor of a public bar. Pity about that, but I suppose I'll have to live with it. So, anywhere then. Where do you recommend?"

"I suggest the bed in my bedroom," Gary said. "Or in your brother's room if he happens to be occupying my room with Rob. Or else in the guest room that's been earmarked for you."

"Bit tame though," Mark said, sounding a little disappointed. "Like being back at home. Whereas here we are in Oxford. There's riverbanks—like where you and David do it—I know that 'cause David told me. "Or," a thought appeared to strike him, "we could do it standing up in the street. You could do me up against a wall. Bet you haven't done that with David."

Actually that was true. Gary had never done it up against a wall with anyone. He made a mental note to remedy the omission with David some time soon. On the other hand, doing it in a more or less public place with this kid... It was just too dangerous to consider. And yet...Gary felt his cock stirring in his jeans. He wondered if Mark really did have his dick out under the table, stiff. He found himself impatient now to see it.

But not quite as impatient as Mark was. He drained the last of his beer. "Let's go," he said. "It's nice just walking in the dark old streets. We could—er—sort of stroll around a bit and see what happened. Couldn't we?"

Laughing, Gary nodded his acceptance, drained down his own glass and got to his feet. "If you have got your cock out," he told Mark, "then for god's sake put it away before you stand up. I'm not walking to the door with you if you've got a little erection poking out of your flies."

"Or even a big one," Mark said. He made a movement under the table and stood up. He was perfectly respectably zipped up, Gary was relieved to see. But he wasn't displeased to see a promising looking bulge in the boy's crotch: a quite long and substantial ridge, in the ten o'clock position. Gary permitted himself a comment. "You dress to the right, I see."

They walked out into the balmy air of an evening that spoke of an Indian summer still lingering in this early autumn term. Along Cornmarket Street (the Corn), up Longwall Street and then left into the long and winding lane, dark and unpeopled, that is called Queen's Lane at one end but has metamorphosed into New College Lane by the time you get to the other. Both sides of the lane were formed by high stone walls of great antiquity, protecting the grounds of the colleges that lay behind them. At intervals there were streetlamps, which shone dimly, their light-pools not quite extending far enough to overlap their neighbors' and so leaving little pockets in between them of relative darkness.

"Should have had a piss before we left the pub," Mark announced. "Need to go now." And he began to fiddle with his flies.

"Me too," said Gary and began to unzip his own. It was true that he too needed to pee, but he was also pleased that the time had come to catch a glimpse of Mark's young cock at last and—to be honest—he would enjoy showing off his own at the same time.

But Mark surprised him beyond all expectation. He didn't just unzip, but pulled his jeans—no underwear lay beneath them—about halfway down his thighs all in one go, so that out sprang his dick, he revealed his sturdy tight-furled balls, and at the same time he exposed his pretty bottom to the night air. And of all those revelations, the greatest—and the greatest surprise— was the size of young Mark's cock. Which (no surprise here, though) had popped out fully stretched and hard and at once was pissing, like a fire hose.

"My god, you're massive!" Gary blurted out. It was true. Never had he seen such a heavyweight piece of apparatus attached to so small a body. Back at school, he had been more than impressed by his roommate, Chris, who, at the age of sixteen, had sported a dick that was out of all proportion to his body size. But this boy's equipment knocked Chris's impressive dimensions into the proverbial cocked hat. Mark's cock was considerably bigger than Gary's own. (Which meant it was bigger than Mark's brother David's, since that—give or take a foreskin—was the twin of Gary's.) It was as big, at least, as the two biggest numbers he'd been privileged to handle: they'd belonged to Martin, the one-time head boy of his school, and to Michel, boyfriend of his former fuck-buddy, Pete. Perhaps Michel's had had the edge where length was concerned. He'd boasted eight and a half inches, and Mark probably didn't have that (yet). But its girth at the base was far in excess of anything Michel could boast of, even at maximum stretch. No wonder David had stopped letting Mark fuck him a year or two ago.

Standing next to his young friend, Gary aimed his stiff prick at the wall and fired the contents of his bladder down its tube. "Why does it always come out in a twist?" Mark asked him. "I mean, like a drill bit. Do you think our cock tubes are rifled on the inside, like guns?"

"I don't know the answer to that," said Gary, as they both continued to fire their fat cocks, like giant water pistols, at the wall.

"Anyway," Mark said conversationally, even before he'd finished pissing, "your prick's looking pretty splendid too, fore-skin or no foreskin. While we're both standing here with our pants down, why don't you make my day and give it to me from behind?"

Gary might have stamped on the idea as recently as two minutes ago. But now, with this delectable boy showing off his arse, balls, thighs and stiff cock right beside him—and with his own jeans sliding down his thighs as he finished peeing and his cock rose fully to the occasion—he was unable to resist the renewed invitation. Standing cocks are strangers to circumspec-tion. After no more than the quickest look around to check the lane was empty he moved round behind Mark, then pulled both their pairs of jeans right down till they snagged around their ankles. He gave an approving glance at Mark's pert, strong calves. Then, spitting on his hand and applying that to his dick for want of other lubrication, he prepared to insert his twitching member inside the younger lad. He was acutely conscious of the fact that, in common with Mark, he'd never fucked anyone standing up against a wall before, let alone done it in the street.

Gary had a vivid memory of his fuck-buddy Peter giving Michel a fine rogering against his bedroom wall two years before. Peter had had to stand on tiptoe in order to get his not-very-long prick up inside the taller Michel. But now, here, the condition was the opposite. Mark's hole was located some three inches nearer the ground than the base of Gary's now-stargazing dick, and he had to bend at the knees in order to push the long thing in. Mark meanwhile had to place the palms of his two hands against the wall to prevent himself (and more particularly his exposed erection) being crushed against it once Gary started thrusting. This had one negative side effect. As Mark put it himself: "Bugger. I can't wank myself."

"Don't worry, kid," said Gary, poking about to find Mark's back entrance. "As soon as I'm properly in, I'll look after that." And just as he finished speaking he popped quickly and easily into Mark, almost by accident.

"Ow," said Mark. Then, "Oh, wow, that feels so lovely."

It felt lovely to Gary too, snug and warm in Mark's inside. "I'll have to get on with it, though," he said a bit apprehensively, as he began to thrust away urgently, using his bent knees as levers, "before anyone comes round the corner." He had begun to be anxious again about being seen. Someone was sure to appear. His heart was beating like a drum. Really, this was insane. He reached round and grabbed Mark's big cock—that action shook the final sparkling drops of water from it—and began to move his hand up and down the thick shaft, feeling Mark's foreskin slippery-sliding back and forth as he did so, in rhythm with his own thrusts but, of necessity, in contrary motion.

"Oh, my god," Gary said half a minute later, still pumping away. "Here come some people now!" Mark was able to look half round and could see three or four young men approaching in the distance. But before either of them could take any decision about either carrying on or rapidly disengaging, stuffing away and buttoning up, the figures had disappeared through an archway in the wall, apparently without having spotted the copulating pair in the shadows.

Perhaps it was that brush with danger that did it. Seconds later, Gary felt his cock preparing to shoot, and at the same time Mark called out, "Oh, Gary, I'm coming," and he immediately sprayed out his load, like lengths of white string in the light of the streetlamps, all over Gary's hand and against the wall, as well as down into his dropped jeans. Gary was very touched that Mark had called out his name as he came. It hastened his own ejaculation, and he returned the compliment as he shot his hot flood deep into his new little friend. "Mark, Mark," he said. "This is for you. A big welcome to Oxford."

Even as he was speaking, they both realized that two more people had come round the corner from the other end of the lane. And stopped. They were two blond young men in identical blue jeans and short denim jackets. Gary and Mark, looking over their shoulders at them, froze in terror. But the twins smiled. Unbelievably to Gary, one of them said, "Don't stop on our account," and the other one, "Keep it up."

"I think we've finished, actually," said Gary nervously, still almost unable to believe this conversation was taking place. His slippery cock came plopping out from between Mark's rosy bumcheeks as he spoke. One of the twins giggled. "That's nice," he said. "Welcome to Oxford." And then they walked on past, with no further comment, while Mark and Gary hastily pulled up their jeans and zipped. They stared after the twins as they receded down the lane. From beneath the backs of their denim jackets hung the tails of two identical striped shirts.

When they arrived back at Gary's and David's shared staircase, the light was showing under David's door. Without knocking, Gary and Mark walked in. A very startled David and Rob leapt to their feet, up from the chairs they'd been sitting in, enjoying a (presumably postcoital) glass of wine. They had good reason to look disconcerted. Neither of them was wearing anything except a T-shirt. Naked from the waist down, and with their cocks seeming unsure whether to be erect or not (they were waving slowly up and down, Rob's cutely tiny, David's four times its size, like some sort of signalling equipment) they looked like two naughty little boys (especially in little Rob's case) who have been caught doing something rather rude, having taken their trousers right off beforehand in order to do it. They sat down again when they saw who their visitors were and Gary, whose own room this was after all, fetched a couple more wine-glasses for himself and Mark.

"So how did you get on?" David asked the new arrivals.

"You first," countered Gary.

David and Rob, David explained with the ghost of a blush, had spent the evening very cozily pleasuring each other on Gary's bed. Gary and Mark involuntarily glanced toward it: the evidence was still fresh and glistening on the covers. "You didn't tell me," David said to Gary, "that young Rob shoots a load as soon as you look at him. Doesn't even need to be touched." Rob, who would have felt crucified by this announcement just a week ago, now merely grinned. "But then he can do it again and again in the space of minutes." As Gary knew. Rob shot tiny loads from his miniature equipment but could do so with a frequency Gary had never encountered before.

Which sort of evened things up. "What about you?"

Mark answered. "Your friend Gary fucked me in the street. In New College Lane, up against that long stone wall. Those two blond twins that Gary says you keep running into were just in time to witness the end and offered their congrats."

There was an astonished silence. "You are joking," David finally said.

"I'm afraid," said Gary, "it's all true."

"Including the twins?"

"Yup."

There was a further silence. Rob broke it. "Well at least we know now—about the twins I mean. What we always guessed."

Gary changed the subject fractionally. "You never told me your little brother has a massive cock."

"I thought that might be a nice surprise for you," David answered smoothly. "Yes, he does indeed."

"In which case, can we have a look at it?" Rob asked Mark cheekily. "Since you're sitting there casting your eyes over mine."

Never the bashful one, Mark stood up and dropped his jeans, lifting up his shirtfronts so Rob could get the whole picture. He was impressively erect, his cockhead peeping from its protecting foreskin, big drum-tight balls framed in a shock of curly pubic hair—quite a big shock, on someone of his age. Gary noticed that Mark's jeans, around his ankles for the second time in an hour, were now in quite a mess, what with Mark's spunk and other dribblings at the front, and some signs that Gary's come had begun seeping out of the boy at the rear.

Rob stood up, meaning to take Mark's organ in his hand, but was caught out by his usual party trick of suddenly letting slip his load. "Oh, no," he said, though with a laugh now, as he felt his semen rise inside him, and the others watched as, before Rob had time to use his hand, his small prick quivered and slightly swelled, causing the glans to peep fractionally from beneath his foreskin, and then sprayed forth three tiny drops like pearls, which landed on the carpet between Mark's feet.

"Never mind, little one," David said, putting one arm around Rob comfortingly, and giving his spent but still pert prick a consoling tweak. "We'll do it properly again soon."

"In which case," Mark asked his brother, "can I go to bed with Gary tonight?" His display now accomplished, and its effect spectacular (on Rob at least), he hauled his jeans back up.

"For tonight only, though," David told him in serious elder brother tones. "I want him back tomorrow night in one piece. All of him."

That didn't mean Mark would have to sleep alone the second and last night of his visit, Gary thought—judging from the interest he'd aroused in Rob.

Gary and Mark left Rob and David, with what remained of the wine, in Gary's room, where they seemed too comfortably ensconced to be dislodged, and made their way upstairs to David's. They undressed fully now, in front of each other, to their mutual delight, then kissed and caressed those parts of each other that they hadn't seen before—as well as some of the ones they already had. Mark was no taller than David, but twice as chunky, despite being two years younger, although no wider than David was around the waist. His upstanding cock incontinently drooled. Speaking more softly than he'd done before, he asked if he might fuck Gary in his brother's bed.

Gary might have been apprehensive, given Mark's dick's impressive girth, but he'd drunk enough not to worry overmuch and besides was delighted to be asked. He showed his consent by lying back, knees raised, legs spread and welcoming the boy on top of him with open arms. For all his puppyish boisterousness before, Mark now entered Gary with care. Moistening his prick with spit was mere courtesy: it already streamed nonstop with precome. Slowly, gently he rodded Gary to and fro, suffusing Gary with flushes of delight and, with the softness of a butterfly, continually kissed his face.

Carried away on clouds of pleasure, Gary was neglecting his own distended cock, and Mark was also too occupied with other things to give it the attention that it craved. Suddenly it did what Gary now thought of as the speciality of Rob and, untouched except by occasional glancing contact with Mark's taut tummy, delivered up a massive load: not Rob's few pretty raindrops though, but a surging flood of cream that made a lake of Gary's belly and chest. Seeing this, Mark said, "Oh, wow, you've come. I'm sorry. I should've wanked you. I forgot." The sight of the milky inundation made him pump his own squirt out, into Gary—a hot transfusion of sperm. Then Mark collapsed forward onto Gary, saying, "Oh, hey, your spunk's still warm, like a bath."

It wouldn't be warm for long, Gary thought practically. Then he realized that he had also pretty much flooded David's bed. Still, that was tit for tat: he remembered the mess David and Rob had made of his own.

To Gary's surprise, Mark fell suddenly asleep after that on Gary's chest, worn out by the novelties of the day. He was still lying in the puddle of Gary's sperm with his cock still firmly plugged into Gary's arse. Gary hadn't the heart to wake him and so they spent most of the night like that. Gary half woke from time to time, to find the boy's prick in varying states: sometimes it felt full and fat, filling the space inside him as a champagne cork is compressed in the neck of its bottle, at others small and slippery like an eel, but always there.

Mark didn't come out of Gary till nearly breakfast time. They masturbated each other briskly before getting up. Then, because of Mark's impending interview at the Divinity School and remembering the state of the boy's jeans, Gary went to borrow a clean pair for him from Rob—they'd be about the right size. He had good reason to hope that Mark would have a successful interview and didn't want anything to go wrong. He would look forward to Mark's coming up to Oxford as a theology student next autumn. Meanwhile Mark could return the borrowed trousers to Rob in the evening. And who knew what might happen then.

HUMP DAY

Dominic Santi

Wednesday was strip night at Chico.

Nobody danced dirtier than Martin. He wore blue silk boxers and black boots. The sweatier he got, the more the slinky fabric clung to his obvious assets. He thrust his hips, rocking back and forth obscenely as he strutted his stuff across the tabletop. His head was buzzed homeboy rough, the short straight bristles spiking up like a stiff, black brush above his glistening brown skin. Even his tattoos gleamed in the flash of the laser lights—EL MONTE across the back of his neck and ropes of barbed wire banded around both his biceps. A steel stud gleamed in his right nipple.

As the hip-hop music throbbed, he put his hands on his ass, arching his pelvis as he thrust out his half-hard cock. His boxers were clinging like a second skin, so damp now the outline of his G-string showed. The audience howled. Martin caught my eye and winked. I raised my beer to him, then slowly lowered the bottle to rub it over my crotch. He grinned, and the bulge in his pants got bigger.

Watching Martin always made me throw a boner. He worked on the same Caltrans night crew I did, flipping his "slow" and "stop" flags at assholes and drunks while I dug up chunks of concrete for the new Los Angeles Metrolink lines. We never talked about Chico at work. The hot topics on our crew were pussy and cars and the Dodgers and pussy. I hadn't known Martin was a fag too until I saw him stripping at Chico. Fuck, he was hot!

Finding Chico made me glad I'd made the move to East L.A. The San Gabriel Valley was no gay Mecca, but I couldn't afford to live in fucking West Hollywood anymore. Even if the commute hadn't been such a bitch, the budget cuts from the fucking recession had cut out all my overtime. My income had dropped below what I'd been making when I'd hired on seven years ago. I was tired and pissed off from another day of trying to sleep in triple-digit temperatures. The AC in my cheap-assed Alhambra apartment didn't work worth shit. My crew had Wednesday nights off. The promise of naked men and cheap Tecate made it worth the Hump Day trip to check out what the website billed as East L.A.'s premier Latin gay bar.

My Irish ass will never pass for Latin, but I was horny and thirsty. I showed my ID to the man at the door and walked into the darkened throb of the crowd beyond—no cover charge. The evening was looking up already. I inhaled deeply, drawing in the scent of hot, sweaty men, letting the tension drain from my shoulders as hip-hop and the sound of Spanglish and deep male laughter seeped into my pores. I made my way to the bar and got a beer then found myself a place along the wall. I leaned back and lifted the bottle, watching the spears of laser light dance across the writhing masses of men as ice-cold beer trickled down my throat.

This was definitely a workingman's bar. Brown-skinned men with shaved heads or short, black hair and ball caps danced in baggy pants and white T-shirts or work shirts embroidered with names like CARLOS or MANNY on the pocket above a company logo. They drank Mexican or cheap domestic beer from the bottle. There wasn't a designer shirt or microbrewed specialty ale in sight. Guys who carried themselves in a way that screamed "cop" were dancing with homeboys or leaning in close enough to damn near rub dicks with gangbangers whose arms and necks were painted solid with tattoos. The few of us there with Anglo skin stuck out like sore thumbs, and nobody seemed to give a shit.

Fuck, this was my kind of bar! I scanned the room, taking in the action. Motorcycle videos played on the huge plasma screen on the wall. A mirror ball flashed over the dance floor. Suddenly, the crowd started hooting. Five dancers had climbed up onto a table, gyrating to the music. The one dancing second from the right had his back to me. Fuck, he had a beautiful ass! It was round and firm, with his baggy pants riding low over satiny blue boxers. His T-shirt clung to the kind of work-toned shoulders I loved to lick. I could almost taste the solid mounds of muscle beneath my tongue: salt and musk. I waited for the dancer to turn around. I had no doubt his pecs and dark brown nipples would draw me like a magnet. I'd grab a handful of ass and lick my way down his glistening six-pack. I'd tongue his cock through those soft, silky boxers. Then I'd turn him around, yank down the fucking pants and bury my face in that gorgeous ass.

I raised my bottle to take another drink. With a jerk of his hips, my dream dancer spun around and started to shimmy. My hand froze halfway to my mouth. *Holy fuck!* The dancer was Martin, the flagman from my crew!

Martin and I had never done more than nod hello at work.

Yeah, I'd noticed his body was fine, despite the hard hat and Day-Glo orange vest and machismo swagger. But there were a lot of guys on our crew, and working nights on the freeway was a bitch. If you didn't pay attention to the job, you could end up dead real quick. But damn! If Martin had ever moved like that at work, I sure as fuck would have paid more attention.

The bulge in the front of his pants that night was as pretty as his ass. His T-shirt clung like a second skin. Nipple rings? It was hard to tell from this far back. Starting at the far left, the dancers started to strip. As each one got down to a G-string or jock, he danced to the edge of the table. People surged forward, tucking bills under straps and into pouches. Martin was fourth.

By then, I'd worked my way to within ten feet of the table. The floor vibrated with sound. Martin cocked his hip and drew his T-shirt over his head. Streaks of red laser light played over his smooth brown skin as whistles split the air. He flexed and ran his hands over his chest, stroking the intertwined male symbols tattooed high on the right side. Light gleamed from the silver bar piercing the nipple below. He swiveled his hips, and those baggy fucking homeboy pants plunged to the top of the table. The crowd roared as he turned and spanked his ass.

With a quick jerk, he pulled his pants free of his boots. Fuckin' breakaway pants! Martin rocked his hips, bumping and grinding. He turned toward me again, the short, thick snake in his crotch taking on a life of its own as he pranced around the stage. He teased his fingers along the waistband of those sexy blue boxers. With one quick tear, they were gone, too!

He worked his way around the table, smiling his wicked handsome grin as people stuffed bills in his G-string. His eyes got huge when he saw me. I held up a twenty—and waited. He rocked his crotch a couple of beats, watching me back. Then he grinned and cocked his hip toward me. I stuffed the bill in the front of his G-string, so he'd feel my cool green money on his dick as he wiggled his hips. Then I motioned for him to turn around.

He dipped and wiggled his ass, flexing those firm, tight globes as he sneered over his shoulder. But his eyes were sparkling. I stuffed another twenty deep in his crack, right up against his asshole. Then I thrust my hips at him, rubbing my beer bottle over my crotch, never breaking eye contact as my dick stretched out into my jeans. I was going to fuck Martin's ass. I knew it, and I was making damn sure he knew it, too.

I nodded toward the wall where I was going to be waiting when he eventually climbed off the table, which was pretty damn quick after that. The last dancer had brought a whole slew of friends, so the competition wound up pretty fast.

Martin's boxers were back on when he joined me. He was carrying two Tecates. He handed me one.

"Didn't know you were a fag," he grinned.

"Same," I smiled back, raising my bottle to him. "I'm going to fuck that pretty round ass."

"Yeah," he laughed, taking a long, slow drink. "But first we're gonna dance."

We danced until they closed the place down. Then I took him out for breakfast, and we went back to my place. His kisses tasted like beer and chorizo. The smooth brown skin of his chest and ass and the hot flesh of his thick uncut cock were everything that looks had promised and more. We fucked and sucked until dawn, then we collapsed in each other's arms on the bed. My AC still didn't work worth shit, and it was still hotter than hell, but I asked him to spend the day anyway. We fucked again when we woke up and once more, after dinner, before we went to work.

* * *

Martin and I still don't talk about dick on the job. But we hang out at lunch, and we catch the Dodgers games together. Sometimes we even catch a matinee on days when we want to sleep in AC that fucking works. And every Wednesday night, we go to Chico. Every Wednesday night, I tip his hot homeboy ass while he dances. Then I take him home and fuck him till we both hear the fucking angels sing. The San Gabriel Valley won't ever be WeHo. But thanks to Chico, East L.A. is now my kind of place. And I fuckin' love it.

I SUCKED OFF AN IRAQI SNIPER

Natty Soltesz

When I was a sophomore in college I got a job bussing tables at a Syrian restaurant. One of the cooks was named Hannad and he was from Iraq. He scared the shit out of me. He was built like a brick shithouse, with crude tattoos lining his hands and powerful arms. He had a handsome but rough face, and he was missing some of his teeth.

He made no effort to hide his dislike of me. Every time I came back into the kitchen he would fix me with an intense, hostile gaze. He told people that he'd been a sniper in the Iraqi Army. I had no doubt that he'd killed—you could see it in his eyes—and I was a skinny, white, gay boy who'd never done anything worse than shoplifting. I dreaded every encounter with him.

I worked there for more than three years and eventually I became a waiter, which meant a lot more interaction with Hannad, and I guess we reached a sort of truce. He wasn't my friend, but he wasn't set on intimidating me anymore, either.

Then one night I was out at a bar with some friends when I

spotted him off in the corner. Feeling bold because I was buzzed, I walked over to him and said hi. We started having an actual conversation, and I realized, as it got later and we got drunker, that he was flirting with me. He pointed to a girl in a red dress, said something about the color red then showed me, by lowering the waistband of his nylon pants, that he was wearing red underwear. It was a pretty obvious overture and it made me half hard. When the bar let out he said, "You come with me."

I thought we'd go back to his place but instead he took me to a diner, like we were on some weird date. He said that there were Iraqi men who performed songs about loving young boys. I was twenty-one at the time, but I had a boyish, innocent look, and I guess he responded to that.

We went back to his apartment and ended up on his bed. I rubbed his soft dick through the crotch of his pants. As he got erect he kissed me roughly. He was all brute strength, throwing me back on the bed and holding me down with one arm while he stripped. He took out his cock, which wasn't anything spectacular but was hard. I blew him for a while, and then he wanted to fuck me. I wasn't used to getting fucked, but I was too afraid to say no to him, so I let him hold me back on the bed and toss my legs over my head. He did not take his time—it hurt like hell. He was rough and unforgiving, and after a while I had to make him stop. I finished by sucking him off and letting him cum all over my face.

After that night, we got along famously. He drafted me as his workout partner and I joined his gym. After my first weight-lifting lesson we went back to his place and sat on the couch, pleasantly tired and weak muscled. He put on some porn, and eventually I reached over to feel his erect cock. I took it out— it was dank and sweaty—and leaned over to blow him. I had more fun this time; I felt more relaxed with him. I held on to his balls—he wouldn't let me get anywhere near his ass—and sucked his little cock for all it was worth. He blew a load in my mouth, and all the while a cheesy studio portrait of him and his girlfriend beamed down at us from the mantel.

The next time, we'd been out drinking and had gone back to his place even though his girlfriend was home. He had a couch and a TV set up in the basement, and I got on my knees before him there and sucked his cock and swallowed his cum while his girlfriend slept upstairs.

One time I was with him when he fucked a girl. He wanted me to join in, but I just wasn't into it. I got behind him and watched him fuck. He had his boxer shorts on but I pulled them down so I could look at his muscled ass. He hated that. He pulled them up but I just pulled them back down, watching his firm butt thrusting while I jacked off and came into my hand.

He fucked me once more, this time after a party at his apartment where the only guests were me and an extremely drunk straight friend of his. After his friend passed out Hannad took me into the bedroom and bent me over. I was more into the idea of getting fucked than I had been the first time, but I still couldn't take it for very long. I was (and still am) a lousy bottom; it just took me a while to realize it.

Through it all we became genuine friends. He told me sad stories about Iraq, like how they used to drug him when he was in Saddam's army to make him a better killer. He'd come to America when the U.S. Army recruited him after the first Gulf War, but he missed Iraq badly. I was with him in the weeks leading up to the 2003 invasion of Iraq, and he was visibly, understandably disturbed. I lost contact with him when I changed jobs. Last I heard he made it back to Iraq, and I sure hope he's okay. Underneath all his aggression he was a genuinely sweet guy who'd been through enough.

I DREAMT

Shane Allison

I dreamt of getting finger-fucked. I dreamt of pierced nipples. I dreamt that my asshole was the size of a tennis ball. I dreamt of leather cock rings and big pink dicks. I dreamt I was bound with extension cord, gagged with stinking, sweaty socks. I dreamt of Jeff Mann raping my butt. I dreamt I was gagging off his cum. I dreamt I drank his piss. I dreamt of frat boy circle jerks, all those dicks coming on my face. I dreamt of passing my ass around to gangbangers and liking it. I dreamt of musky white Irish asses and bathhouse floors slippery with semen. I dreamt of well-hung go-go boys, dollar bills hanging from their G-strings. I dreamt of Tom sucking peanut butter and Cheez Whiz off my dick. I dreamt that I was drenched in piss. I dreamt of the asses of biker dudes hanging out of leather chaps. I dreamt that my face was being smothered in ripe armpits. I dreamt of calloused hands of brutes tugging at my hips. I dreamt of one big brute dick after another taking it out on my ass. I dreamt of jacking off with chocolate sauce.

I dreamt of getting fisted by old men. I dreamt of cum being licked out of the assholes of gay porn stars. I dreamt of lean, lithe Chelsea boys. I dreamt of blond fur around assholes. I dreamt of shaved balls and thick strings of cum in beards. I dreamt I had a fetish for the gym shorts of sweaty teenage boys. I dreamt I was getting the best blow job ever. I dreamt of a butt plug slathered with Vaseline. I dreamt that I found a white hair in my pubes. I dreamt that there was nine inches of dick past these lips. I dreamt that my ass was raw and tender from a spanking Simon gave me and afterward he fucked me till I saw stars. I dreamt of Emanuel's warm asshole. I dreamt that my daddy caught me jacking off while I watched gay porn.

I dreamt that Chris had orange hair. I dreamt that I ate his ass so good, his toes curled. I dreamt of my lips around his dick. I dreamt that he was smiling sadistically at me as I blew him. I dreamt I had a pussy. I dreamt of the sweet foreskin of Latino men. I dreamt of beefy, bubbled asses. I dreamt of asses with beauty marks, birthmarks and freckles. I dreamt of pimpled asscheeks too. I dreamt of dicks hanging from the zippers of a farmer's overalls. I dreamt of teardrop piss slits and dick heads glossy with lubricant. I dreamt of French tickler rubbers and the scuffed knees of Brazilian boys. I dreamt of giving blow jobs in the bathrooms of college libraries. I dreamt of Dean's sweaty ass. I dreamt of whips, cuffs and alligator tit clamps. I dreamt of wet, naked men toweling off in Montgomery Gym showers, dicks hanging for the attention of a man's mouth. I dreamt I drugged some Mexican boy and fucked him while he was unconscious. I dreamt of cocks being shoved under dividers. I dreamt of a butt cupped in hands as it rode a stiff dick. I dreamt of that same stiff dick bulging in tight jeans. I dreamt of hands forcing my head in stinking baseball stadium pissers. I dreamt of buttcheeks like valleys. I dreamt of giving head in the bathrooms of mall food courts. I dreamt of the warm mouth of a married construction worker. I dreamt of a cute twink in camouflage cutoffs. I dreamt of thick lips on white boys. I dreamt that I was getting fisted by Robert Mapplethorpe. I dreamt of punks and skater boys with tattooed cocks. I dreamt of perfectly pedicured toes being sucked and worshiped. I dreamt of standing on toilets, watching the action overhead from my stall. I dreamt of cum being spat out in a pool of commode water. I dreamt of teeth brown from chewing tobacco behind a handlebar mustache. I dreamt of dicks sweeter than pussy. I dreamt of muscular bicycle thighs, cum sticky in crotch hair. I dreamt of rim chairs. I dreamt of dick rings. I dreamt of slurped boners. I dreamt of sweaty balls stuffed in my mouth. I dreamt of sugar daddies that would pay me anything for a good time.

I dreamt of daddy-bear dick up my Floridian butt. I dreamt of big bellies and flat asses. I dreamt of enemas filled with a trucker's piss. I dreamt of Doug's pierced dick. I dreamt of the steel clanging against my molars. I dreamt that I was bound and gagged by Catholic priests. I dreamt I was the prison bitch of a white supremacist. I dreamt of writing endless poems about Jarret's dick until my fingers bled. I dreamt of being tied up, slapped around. I dreamt of Jonathan saying, "Suck that cock." I dreamt of a guy coming through a glory hole. I dreamt Ma found my stash of porn mags in my desk, and I woke up in a cold sweat. I dreamt of eating the ass of my American Lit. professor. I dreamt of waistbands of boxers showing from the waistlines of jeans. I dreamt of abducting men, throwing them in my van with tinted windows, taking them to a place no one knows about and raping their mouths and butts. I dreamt of well-hung insurgents. I dreamt of giving terrorists blow jobs in exchange for the lives of passengers on United 93. I dreamt of swallowing Bush's poisonous Republican semen if he would give up the presidency. I dreamt of sucking off Hitler in order to save the lives of millions of Jews. I dreamt of eating his ass if he promised to close the concentration camps. I dreamt of the sweaty assholes of Iranian soldiers. I dreamt of drinking piss to save the lives of gay Iraqis.

I dreamt of cowboys in ten-gallon hats with ten-inch dicks. I dreamt of a doctor armed with latex gloves exploring my asshole. I dreamt of semen staining the wedding rings of married men. I dreamt of offering blow jobs to L.A. gangs in exchange for automatic weapons. I dreamt of a hairy ass under panty hose. I dreamt of balls banging against my butt. I dreamt I was lying naked on a bed of black leather jackets. I dreamt of a stark-raving mad scat queen. I dreamt of James Franco naked on a poster. I dreamt of shooting off in a white tube sock. I dreamt of belt buckles clanging against tiled floors. I dreamt of hands pushed down into slacks. I dreamt that my dick was thicker than a kielbasa sausage. I dreamt of jacking off under my bedcovers. I dreamt of puckered rectums. I dreamt of stainless steel dildos and chain restraints. I dreamt of Matt all macho and butch. I dreamt of being pimped out to dirty truckers. I dreamt of legs being propped upon shoulders while getting fucked. I dreamt of all the countless assholes I've rimmed. I dreamt of video cameras hidden in my bedroom closet. I dreamt of boys talking dirty to me in Brazilian accents. I dreamt of nipples bigger than dinner plates. I dreamt of snorting coke off the torsos of twinks in a Burger King bathroom.

I dreamt of well-hung dicks with lots of veins. I dreamt that Anthony shot off on my green bedroom carpet. I dreamt that Bobby and I were high and drunk. One thing led to another and before I knew it, I was sucking his dick. I dreamt of Michael's country butt. I dreamt of Jared screaming when I shoved the first couple of inches of dick up his ass. I dreamt that Quentin gave me teeth while he blew me. I dreamt I was fucked up on coke and booze while getting fucked by total strangers.

I dreamt of pretty light-skinned dicks. I dreamt of gorgeous Cuban cocks. I dreamt of puddles of piss on the floors of sex clubs. I dreamt that my ass was sprinkled with baby powder. I dreamt of smoked link sausages, bananas, cucumbers, carrots, corn dogs and dill pickles. I dreamt my asscrack was wet with spit and sweat. I dreamt of the muscles of security guards tight under blue polyester. I dreamt that I was spread-eagle in the back rooms of leather bars, nameless, faceless men waiting to fuck my butt. I dreamt that I was bent over a spanking bench, ten to twenty lashes across my ass with a leather riding crop. I dreamt of standing in a pit, men gathered around me and spitting in my mouth. I dreamt I was puking cum under a plum tree. I dreamt that I was such a cum slave. I dreamt that my tongue was down a drag queen's throat. I dreamt of nipple rings. I dreamt that my dick was slathered with coconut-scented hair grease.

I dreamt of hard dicks in smoke-gray warm-ups. I dreamt of Omair's long, curly hair. I dreamt I kissed the purple scar above Surachart's groin. I dreamt I was jacking off to Matty jacking off naked on his bed. I dreamt of Noel's ass in the air as he blew his boyfriend, Eric. I dreamt of sniffing Daniel's sweaty shorts after a long jog. I dreamt of soap lather trickling down into his German pubes. I dreamt of blowing my professors for an *A*. I dreamt of dicks that curved in a weird way. I dreamt of having phone sex with this guy I went to high school with. I dreamt that I was getting blown on a park picnic table by a cross-dresser. I dreamt of a young black boy naked on the toilet, jacking off. I dreamt of old men cruising for dick in stalls. I dreamt of a single blue eye looking at me through a glory hole. I dreamt of junior high locker rooms that smelled of ass. I dreamt of monks naked under their robes.

I dreamt of big-dick Chippendale dancers. I dreamt of rimming Paul's ass, drunk off coconut rum in my dream. I dreamt of sucking off Ishmael in an orange stall. I dreamt of someone's cum trickling down my arm. I dreamt of slurping boners. I dreamt of cum on lips. I dreamt that I sucked off three dicks in a bathroom infamous for cruising. I dreamt you took it out on my flesh. I dreamt of strawberry tongues lapping at musky assholes. I dreamt I had a dick of death. I dreamt of dick-cheese curdled in a blanket of foreskin. I dreamt of fist-fucking, my arm all the way up some guy's ass to the elbow. I dreamt I was sucking Bryan off in the front seat of my car. I dreamt I was shrimping toes. I dreamt I was getting off on the smell of men's underwear. I dreamt there was something sticky on my belly. I dreamt of you feeding me Belgian waffles in bed, Matt. I dreamt of macho butch boys taking it out on my flesh. I dreamt of a pair of lips that curved just so. I dreamt of a firm ass in tight black jeans. I dreamt of gagging off a dick in a dark booth that reeked of fresh cum.

I dreamt of being cock-teased in a gym shower. I dreamt that I tapped my foot and got a blow job for it. I dreamt of being surrounded by huge Blatino dicks. I dreamt that all these men that cruised tearooms lusted after me and no one else. I dreamt of college-age hard-ons. I dreamt that I was slathered in grape jelly. I dreamt that I was picking blond pubic hairs off my tongue. I dreamt that I had a knife held to my throat while being raped. I dreamt of an ass tightening around my dick. I can't remember what he looked like. I dreamt of toothless silver daddies giving me good head. I dreamt of nappy pubic hairs. I dreamt of silk panties soft across my dick and balls. I dreamt of Chelsea boys prying my asscheeks apart. I dreamt of cum dripping from a married man's lips. I dreamt of bloodshot blue eyes staring up at me, a mouth filled with dick. I dreamt that I was hung like a donkey. I dreamt I was a porn star. I dreamt I could fit two dicks up my ass. I dreamt of all these men standing in line waiting to fuck me. I dreamt I was in a hot basement with lots of men, all of them grabbing at each other's dicks. I dreamt of an ass that was as white as milk. I dreamt of a place that stank of poppers. I dreamt that James Franco and I were fuck-buddies. I dreamt that I was handcuffed naked to my bed with an anal plug up my ass. I dreamt I was slathered in Crisco. I dreamt that a wrinkled ass was bent to my dick. I dreamt of wet, sticky fingers traipsing along my lips. I dreamt of cum trickling down stall walls. I dreamt that I was being fucked good and hard. I dreamt that someone was fucking me nice and slow. I dreamt of a black dildo being shoved up a white ass. I dreamt I came in Travis's mouth when he told me not to. I dreamt of big balls in my face. I dreamt of uncut dicks with mushroom heads. I dreamt of supple buttcheeks. I dreamt that I was pulling some hustler's hair as I fucked him. I dreamt I was in a porn video sucking dicks to the balls. I dreamt I was getting gang-banged by she-males. I dreamt of getting an anonymous blow job in the basement of an adult video store. I dreamt of grown men dressed in diapers and bonnets.

I dreamt I was getting married in the gym of my old high school with an '80s prom theme: him the famous quarterback, me wearing a pretty white dress and a tiara and holding a big bouquet of roses.

BAREBACKING

Simon Sheppard

In the beginning, you didn't mean to. Not at all. But there you were, with a condom around your rapidly deflating dick and a beautiful brown Indian man in your bed. The Indian's hole was, as usual, tight, and the guy had already told you that he'd thought you two had fucked raw before, a few months back. Which wasn't true. Whatever.

You were virtually certain your partner was negative; you knew damn well that you yourself were. You peeled off the condom and threw it on the floor. Squirting a little more lube on your dick, you began sliding your hard-on against the man's warm, welcoming ass. Your cock instantaneously grew hard, harder than it had been all night.

It had been so many years, so long since you'd had unprotected sex. The Indian guy turned over on his stomach, the way he always liked to get fucked.

It was easy, amazingly easy, to slide inside. For the first time since you'd started screwing the guy, it seemed like there was no resistance, no fight. *This is so wrong,* you thought, but that didn't stop you from sliding all the way in and staying there. Considering the number of times you had fucked the fellow—a married man whose wife (pronounced, in the Indian fashion, "vife," providing a little cross-cultural thrill) was often out of town—this time felt surprisingly unfamiliar. Luxurious, that was the word for it. *Luxurious.*

You raised yourself up on your extended arms and looked down at the broad brown back. Sliding your dick in and out, in and out, you couldn't believe how totally, absolutely, fantastically great it felt.

Well, strictly speaking, that wasn't true. You *could* believe it, easily. It was, after all, how sex had once been supposed to feel, but at the same time it was as if the two of you had a dirty little secret, one neither of you would ever tell.

The Indian man had always been, in fact, a great, hungry bottom once his hole had loosened up. But now, skin on skin, there had been no initial tightness, no gradual ramping up of pleasure, and it took an effort of will not to come too soon. You would have liked to switch positions, to get the guy on his back, look down at his handsome face, kiss him. But it was what it was: the guy didn't kiss, and he preferred it from behind. So you pounded away, enjoying what surely must be a once-only raw fuck.

You were so very, very happy.

"You're not going to come inside me, right?"

"Of course not." You didn't mention you'd already felt yourself leaking precum deep inside his ass.

Pretty soon you sensed yourself reaching the point of no return. "I'm gonna come," you said, pulling your slick cock out of the well-used hole, looking down to watch the naked shaft sliding out. Without even having to touch yourself, you shot off all over the man's back, milky sperm on chocolate skin. You caught your breath, then rolled off your partner.

The just-fucked man turned over, a big smile on his face. His dark cock was still fully hard. He reached down and stroked himself till his nut sac, nearly black, tightened, pumping a big load out onto his belly.

"I loved when you fucked me," the man said. He had never used the word "love" before, in any context.

"Me too," you said. "A lot." *I won't be doing that again,* you thought.

On your way home from the Indian's, the warm spring night seemed full of possibilities, the fragrance of night-blooming jasmine for once not cloying but absolutely perfect.

You stopped into an all-night doughnut place, braving the fluorescents, and got an apple fritter, still hot out of the oven, and a cup of coffee. The caffeine would keep you up till dawn, but that was okay; no work the next day. You bit into the smooth, sweet dough. Life was, indeed, good.

If you *had* done something dangerous, you had no idea what it had been.

A couple of weeks later, after you'd fucked your buddy a couple more times, both without a condom, the Indian man's wife returned and further fucking was, for the moment, off. Even your emails went unanswered.

For a week or so after that, unmanageably horny, you jacked off two or three times a day, but one night you decided to throw caution pretty much to the winds and answer an ad you'd seen online.

When your correspondent came over, he was even better looking than he'd looked in the photo he'd emailed—a very pleasant surprise. In his midtwenties, the guy's face was pretty and unlined, his hair long and blondish, his handlebar mustache a waxed-up architectural achievement that framed his big, soft-looking lips.

"My name's Marc, with a *c*," he said.

You hadn't even gotten to the bedroom when you started tearing each other's clothes off. Marc, sensing a belt-unbuckling problem, undid his own jeans and pulled them halfway down, revealing blue-checked boxers.

It was gratifying, when you reached down and groped through the cotton fabric, to discover that Marc's cock was small, thin and very hard. Contrary to what you supposed you were supposed to prefer, you actually had a thing for little dicks, and it was exciting to you that this lovely, slightly overweight young man had one.

Once Marc had thoroughly stripped down, his body plump, a bit furry and otherwise desirable, it turned out that he also had an edible-looking, perfectly pink hole.

"Get on the bed, on your back, legs up," you said, and once Marc had done exactly that, hands grabbing ankles to keep his legs in the air, you hungrily dived right in. You really loved eating ass. Loved it past the point of explanation, of reason. Even at the height of your caution, you'd always rimmed asses—and, amazingly, had never suffered more than an upset tummy as a result of your passions.

After you'd sated yourself, you backed off, wiped your mouth and spit-lubed your dick. This time, unlike the first bare fuck with the Indian, there was no hesitation. Marc had advertised for a raw fuck, and a raw fuck was what he was going to get.

He had warned you by email that his hole was tight, but it wasn't, not really, though in any case, the extended rimming had prepped it well. Just a little prodding, and there it was: the feeling of skin sliding against skin. Well, it was against mucous membrane really, but that sounded a lot less romantic, and with your dick all the way inside Marc, your pubic bone pressing up against the boy's meaty ass, you weren't about to quibble over terminology.

"I'm getting a cramp in my leg," Marc said.

"Want to ride me, instead?"

"Sure."

You rearranged yourselves, Marc on top and straddling you, hole against hard cockhead. With one swift stroke, Marc lowered himself down on you, velvety hot softness enveloping your sensitive shaft.

You looked up at Marc's handsome face, at the cute mustache, the bright blue eyes, the skinny little dick oozing precum, and though you knew you were expected to keep fucking for a good long time, you realized you were, distressingly, already at the point of no return.

"Fuck, I'm going to come," you said.

If Marc was disappointed, he hid it well. "Go for it," he encouraged.

"Inside?" It had been prearranged, so you didn't really need permission, or if you did, it was your own permission to yourself.

"Yeah."

The spasms came from deep inside your balls, and they lasted for a long, long time, until you'd shot your entire load of sperm inside Marc's furry ass. Marc leaned over, allowing your dick to slide out of his ass. Though he'd said in his emails that he didn't kiss, Marc planted a surprising soft kiss on your mouth; that mustache felt great.

"Can I ask you a favor, Marc?"

"Sure, I think."

You'd been wanting to do this for a decade, more. "Let me eat your ass a little more."

When Marc was obligingly on all fours, you knelt behind him and spread his asscheeks. As the hole relaxed, a stream of cum trickled out. You plunged your tongue against it, licking it up.

You jerked away with a shudder. *What the fuck am I doing?* you thought. Then you relaxed, snuggled your face against Marc's ass and slurped some more.

Like any loss of virginity, you reflected, the first time had been the hardest. (Though okay, it hadn't really been the first time, since you had, many years ago, never used rubbers at all.)

But now that you had become almost accustomed to barebacking, nearly reconciled; now that you had found the very perfect Marc, the blond boy wasn't answering your emails; you sent four intentionally breezy notes suggesting you meet up again then, not wanting to seem a pest, not wanting to feel any more rejected than necessary, gave up.

You once had an English boyfriend who'd taught you the phrase, "In for a penny, in for a pound." Though the Euro had made it technically obsolete, in this case it seemed appropriate.

A barebacking party was not, in your city, hard to find.

You hadn't been to a sex party for years, not since you'd brought home a persistent case of scabies. So it was with a certain amount of trepidation that you made your way to the address specified in his invitation.

You were still unsure, actually, just what you'd be prepared to do once you got to the party. Unlike the Indian man and unlike Marc, the men at the party, you assumed, were more likely to fuck first, negotiate afterward. Still, it might be interesting just to walk in the door.

When you paid your entrance fee and walked inside—into a nicely furnished, middle-class house, as it happened, not some sleazy dive—you were pleasantly surprised to find a goodly variety of men already there, some already naked. Out of the couple of dozen guys, there were a few standard-issue gym bunnies; an unclothed older man with a thatch of unexpectedly sexy gray hair on his meaty chest; a young Asian man, Thai maybe, with beautiful eyes and a tight-fitting Lycra wrestling singlet that showed off his hard dick; a prodigiously tattooed, skinny young blond guy with piercings everywhere, including his dick; a black man in Bermuda shorts; a bear or two. And you.

There was an air of sociability mixed with awkward expectancy; some of the men seemed to know each other well, while others hung around on the margins. Then one guy, obviously the organizer/host, announced that the door had been closed to newcomers and detailed the rules for the evening.

You hadn't realized till then what the setup actually was—insufficient research, you supposed. The party was in fact a gangbang, the tattooed boy the planned recipient of everyone else's loads. This was not only not a turn-on for you—you'd planned on a one-on-one, or a threeway at most—but a little worrisome, too. Fucking one ass without a rubber was one thing; plunging your cock into a reservoir of other men's cum, much of it no doubt infected, quite another. It was only after the festivities were already underway that you realized you might have asked to go first, thereby shortening your participation but allaying your fears. By then, though, one of the gym bunnies had groaningly popped a load inside the tattooed boy's ass, his cock quickly replaced by the gray-haired man's.

Meanwhile, some of the men were getting blown—fluffed for their upcoming fucks, no doubt, since oral sex to completion was not the main dish on the menu. The muscular man who just finished fucking was headed your way, his cock still hard, at least probably a testament to the powers of Viagra.

"Drop your pants and I'll blow you," the muscular man said.

With a shock, you realized that you were the only one there who was still fully clothed. You unzipped your fly, took out your half-erect cock and, when the well-built man was on his knees, slipped it between the guy's lips. It felt great, but you still weren't getting fully hard. You didn't think of yourself as a prude—far from it—but there was something slightly disconcerting about watching the older man, having come, pull out of the tattooed boy's slick, dripping hole, to be replaced mere seconds later by the Asian man. Hot, yes, but somehow not quite right.

"The bottom boy..." you began, speaking to no one in particular. The man sucking your cock paused for a minute, though, and looked up.

"Alex? He's a friend of mine. Bug-chaser. He came here for the gift. Been here before, actually, and it looks like he'll keep trying till he gets it."

That was it: enough. Too much, actually.

"Thanks for the head," you said, "but I think I'm going to split."

Taking care to seem casual, you made his way across the room, which already smelled of sweat, cum and ass, and out the front door. You paused for a moment, until you heard the door being locked behind you, then headed home through the chill night air.

A couple of weeks after your abrupt departure from the party, you went to the clinic for the result of your HIV test.

Testing was always an anxiety producing experience for you, but the results were, as expected, negative.

You hadn't barebacked since the party, hadn't had any kind of sex with anyone, actually. Marc, who'd warned you that he didn't play around all that often, hadn't even bothered to reply to your emails. And cruising Craigslist had turned out to be a frustrating pain in the ass. So you'd contented yourself, for the time being, with jacking off, sometimes to the point of soreness.

Then, one sunny morning, you got an email from your Indian friend:

Sorry I haven't got back in touch with you before, but I guess you understand. My wife is out of town again. Want to fuck me? "Bare" went unspoken, but implied.

You remembered the feeling of your unsheathed dick sliding into the caramel-colored man's soft hole, recalled licking your sperm from Marc's ass, thought about skinny little Alex getting gang-banged in a quest for HIV infection.

You reread the email.

Want to fuck me?

It took you a good long while to decide.

SHEL'S GAME

Jonathan Asche

Shel slides his hand down my back, hesitating briefly at the base of my spine to dig his fingers into the hard flesh beneath my shirt before moving to my ass. My jeans are ragged and threadbare, nothing I would have worn out in public. They're reserved for messy household projects, as suggested by the paint splatters and dirt stains. But Shel insisted. "Those pants hug your ass perfectly," he said.

Shel's hand follows the center seam, the one that goes right between my buttcheeks, his fingers gliding over the curve of my ass until they reach the spot where a hole has worn through the fabric. The hole isn't noticeable to the casual eye, but Shel knows it's there and pushes his fingers inside. The hole in my jeans is near *my* hole. I'm not wearing underwear (of course); Shel has easy access.

"Stop it," I scold as his index finger prods my asslips.

"Thought you liked it," he says, smiling, staring straight ahead.

A fingertip works its way past my puckered sphincter, leaving me breathless. My cock swells instantly.

"Not here," I scold.

"Why *not* here?"

The hostess enters the waiting area, bearing two menus and a frozen smile. We follow her to our table, Shel's hand remaining on my ass—and his finger up my hole—the entire time. To think I was embarrassed to be wearing ratty jeans. I cross my hands in front of my crotch to hide my telltale bulge. "Hands by your side," Shel whispers, and I obey.

The restaurant isn't fancy, just fashionable. There are straight and gay diners; some giggle as we pass by, others *tsk tsk*, but most don't seem to notice us, or pretend they don't. By the time we reach our table my face is red hot.

We have a table for two, but rather than sit across from each other, Shel and I settle in side by side, looking out at the restaurant. Shel puts a finger to my lips—the same finger that was digging into my asshole—and tells me I'm cute when I'm embarrassed. I take the finger into my mouth and suck on it loudly, making Shel laugh. A waiter clears his throat and asks if we'd like anything to drink.

After the waiter leaves with our order Shel points out three guys sitting at the bar, in the thirty- to fortysomething range, laughing like they're already on their second round of drinks.

"They're cute," Shel says, not taking his eyes off the men.

"The one with the beard is hot," I say.

Shel's eyes brim with mischief. "I didn't know you had a thing for beards."

And then: "Go up to him and tell him you want to suck his cock." By the tone of his voice I can tell Shel isn't joking.

Excitement and terror wrestle inside my stomach. "I—I can't do that."

Shel slides a hand between my legs and squeezes. My hard-on gives me away. "Yes you can," he says. "You can because you want to."

And Shel wants me to; that's the deciding factor. I get up, trembling, nearly knocking over the candle on the table.

I barely acknowledged Shel when I first saw him six months ago, at a Christmas party. A bald, middle-aged man with a broad, unremarkable face and a stocky build—he looked like someone who'd try to sell me life insurance, I quipped to Aaron, a sinewy cutie I met at the same party. I wasn't interested in meeting him, let alone fucking him. But Shel cornered me in the kitchen when I was freshening my drink. "Don't worry," he said, smiling broadly, "I won't try to sell you insurance. I'm even more exciting: I'm an accountant."

"And I'm a murderer. I'm about to go kill someone," I replied.

"Your friend didn't say anything. I was standing two feet behind you when you said I looked like an insurance agent. Don't be embarrassed. I thought it was funny."

That wasn't all that Shel found funny. I'm sure he finds my present humiliation hilarious.

I wonder if Shel has already arranged this meeting via a chat-room. Nevertheless, the walk to the bar is one of the longest in my life.

I move in to the left of the man with the beard. "Excuse me," I say.

He's talking to his friends, seated on the right. I have to repeat myself before he acknowledges me. "Yes?"

I lean in close. His cologne smells lemony. "I want... I want to suck your cock."

An interminable moment passes before the man responds. He looks at me, thick eyebrows raised, like he's not sure he heard me correctly. His eyes travel down my body and back up to my face. Then the man with the beard smiles.

We meet in the alley behind the restaurant. A sagging chain-link fence separates the alley from a neighboring vacant lot. Clouds hide the moon and there's the chance of rain in the air. Except for a pool of bluish-white light emanating from the security lamp above the restaurant's back door, the alley is dark, ominous—and exciting.

We move behind a Dumpster.

"Take it out." My voice is a whisper over sandpaper.

The bearded guy says, "Why don't you take it out for me?"

On my knees I face the sizeable bulge in his khaki pants. I'm so eager that I rip open his fly, yank down his underwear and pull his cock into the night air.

I'm speechless.

The moment reminds me of the astonishment at seeing Shel's cock for the first time, when I was "dating" Aaron. Aaron took me back to his place, a condo in a luxury high-rise I couldn't imagine someone in his early twenties affording. It wasn't Aaron's place, it turned out. And Aaron wasn't a date; he was *bait*. While I was fucking Aaron, pounding his petite ass doggie-style, in walked the condo's real owner, Shel, a lewd tent pitched in his black silk pajama bottoms.

His intrusion startled me, then pissed me off. Aaron was unfazed, of course: Shel was expected, and Aaron was expecting the middle-aged accountant's cock in his mouth. Shel, ever the gracious host, untied the drawstring to his pajamas and let them fall around his ankles.

"Jesus Christ," I whispered. Shel had the most perfect cock

I'd ever seen: long and thick, crowned with a dark, rosy helmet glistening with precum. The sight of Shel's cock made me forget my initial anger. It made me forget about *Aaron*. I watched Aaron slurp on the older man's fat tool with such obvious delight that all I wanted was to wrap my mouth around that monster and worship it, too.

Just like I want to worship the bearded man's cock now. His cock isn't as thick as Shel's, but it is longer, though not by much. It's also uncut, the foreskin rolled back to reveal a shiny, succulent head. I prod the folds of foreskin with my tongue, and from there I glide along the rim of the cockhead. He watches me intently as I rub his swollen dong across my face, across my mouth. I savor the smoothness of the skin and its vaguely musky smell. A thick drop of precum lands on my cheek, and I rub it in with the crown of his cock. I cup his balls, feeling their weight in my hands. When I nuzzle the hairy scrotum I get another whiff of his manly scent.

I take the cock into my mouth—deep, until the tip of my nose is brushing his pubes and his cockhead is hitting the back of my throat. The man with the beard grunts as if he's just been punched. His grunts become moans as my lips travel up and down that magnificent cock, as my tongue massages the shaft and laves the head.

My own cock is aching with a pain that's as enjoyable as it is excruciating. I want to jack off as I suck this well-hung stranger, but I have to wait for my release. So I keep my hands busy with his prick, one gripping his shaft while the other circles his nut sac and tugs, just enough to make the man's body twitch and his cock pulse.

The space around us becomes crowded and the man suddenly withdraws. His two friends have joined us. One is tall and broad shouldered, with short blond hair retreating from his temples.

He dresses like he wishes he were ten years younger. The other man is tall, slim and looks like he's of Indian descent. His black, curly hair is gelled into submission and small, delicate glasses shield his dark eyes. The men's expressions make it clear their cocks are doing all the thinking, and a glance at their crotches tells me they're thinking real hard.

Behind the two men, in partial shadow, stands Shel.

"Go on," he says, and I return to sucking the bearded man's cock.

The man is self-conscious now, but I quickly make him forget our audience. I swallow his cock in a single, lusty gulp. He cries out and I suck his dick harder, only pulling it out of my mouth to tell him how much I love sucking his cock. He grips my head with his hands, pulling my hair while he fucks my mouth. Thunder rumbles in the distance.

The bearded man announces his orgasm in fast, shallow breaths. "All over his face," Shel says. "Cover his face with your load." I think of that time, months ago, when Shel walked in on Aaron and me, when Aaron sucked Shel's cock until he was rewarded with a thick load that coated the left side of his pretty face. I'd wanted to lick Shel's cockhead clean, but he told me to stay put, to just watch as Aaron gently—lovingly—brushed his tongue against the oozing crown of Shel's prick as the older man stroked Aaron's golden hair. Shel had then looked at me as if he'd just discovered my presence. That's when he told me that if I wanted to taste his load I could lick it off Aaron's face. And I did, happily.

Now I'm about to get my face covered in the bearded man's cum. But he doesn't pull his cock out of my mouth in time, if he intended to at all. The bitter taste erupts in my mouth and I pull back, his exploding cock popping from between my lips. The other men cheer—"Oh, yeah!" "Shoot that load!"—as spunk splatters my chin. I turn my face to catch another splat along my left jaw. The man groans loudly, shaking the last drops from his cock. I lunge forward, grabbing his dick and slurping the jizz off the pulsing head. "*Damn*," says one of the men, sounding simultaneously shocked and impressed. But I'm only interested in impressing one man, and so far he's keeping quiet.

The man with the beard lets out a final, satisfied groan. He smiles at me, shakes his head and steps away, stuffing his cock back into his pants.

I'm sorry to see that cock disappear, but there are two more to take its place. Both the blond and the Indian have pulled out their hard-ons. Their cocks aren't as big as the bearded man's, but I want to suck them all the same. The blond guy's cock is cut, curves in the middle and tapers to a point; it resembles a pink, veined banana. The Indian's dick is two shades darker than the rest of him, except for the plump head, which is a pink-hued tan. Shel remains in the background, wearing a Mona Lisa smile.

The Indian steps up and bats me in the face with his cock. "Stick out your tongue," he hisses. His aggressiveness startles me. Because he wears glasses and—I'm ashamed to admit—because of his ethnicity, I'd expected him to be shy. The Indian squeezes a fat tear of precum onto the tip of my tongue. I want to close my mouth, savor the taste, but he has other ideas. Suddenly, my mouth is filled with his cock.

"Oh, yeah, *suck* it," the Indian sighs.

The blond guy moves in beside his friend, stroking his stiff prick as I suck off the Indian with deep gulps. My arousal is torturous—my cock is really hurting. I reach between my legs to squeeze my crotch, only to hear Shel snap, "Not yet!" I reach instead for the blond guy's cock, playing with it while his friend thrusts his dick down my throat. Lightning crackles through the clouds, chased by thunder.

The restaurant's back door opens. The blond guy spins around, frantically trying to get his cock back into his pants. The Indian freezes, the proverbial deer in headlights. The bearded guy has long since disappeared. A waiter stands in the doorway, an unlit cigarette inches from his lips. It's the same waiter who took our drink order earlier. He's young, well built and as embarrassed as we are.

Correction: as embarrassed as *most of us* are. Shel says, calmly: "Instead of sucking on that cigarette, how about letting my friend suck you."

A beat goes by before the waiter chuckles. He returns the cigarette to its pack and ambles toward us.

I return my attention to the Indian's cock. He's not so aggressive now, the waiter's appearance having broken the sexual spell. Likewise the blond guy remains a little out of sorts, cautiously pulling his cock out into the night air but poised to stuff it back in should someone else surprise us.

Shel, of course, loves surprises, especially if he's the one doing the surprising. Several weeks ago he had a guest from out of town—Loren, a guy he used to work with, about the same age as Shel but, truth be told, a whole lot hotter. On Loren's second night in town, while we were lounging in the living room, chatting after dinner, Shel began discussing what a hot fuck I am. I'm used to Shel bragging, but with Loren he got uncomfortably graphic: "I'll shoot my load into a bowl and he'll lap it up like a dog." Then Shel told me to suck Loren's cock. Loren, already mortified by Shel's conversation, protested. "C'mon, this is going too far."

But Loren never tried to stop me as I unzipped his fly.

Perhaps Shel caught me checking out Loren, or maybe he saw Loren looking me over. Or maybe Shel planned on me sucking off his friend before Loren ever showed up. Regardless, my shock delighted him, perhaps even more than watching his friend cum in my mouth.

Back in the alley, Shel watches as the three men surround me. Once the waiter unzips his black trousers and pulls out his cock—still soft but getting into the spirit of things—the Indian and the blond guy relax.

I move my mouth from the Indian's cock to the blond's, sucking fiercely first one and then the other before switching dicks, leaving them both hard and wanting while I shift my attention to the waiter, who is now hard. His cock is on the skinny side, but what it lacks in girth it makes up for in length. The tip of my tongue bores into the piss slit, and he trembles. I look up at the waiter, and our eyes meet before he looks away. My eyes roll back to his crotch, and my mouth travels down his shaft. I gnaw on the folds of his shaved nut sac, suck on his balls and then quickly return to the head of his cock. He shudders and his cries reverberate down the alley: "Oh, *man*! God*damn*, that's—oh, yeah!"

I return to the Indian, who's resumed the role of sexual aggressor. "Suck my cock," he commands, cupping the back of my head and ramming his dick so deeply down my throat that I gag.

"Oh, shit, I'm gonna cum."

It's the blond, jacking off, losing control. A crack of thunder drowns out his cries as he coats the right side of my face with his load. I turn to him to receive another shot, this one in the center of my forehead. I guide his cock into my mouth for the final spurts, sucking even after he's drained his balls, until he finds the sensation too intense and pushes me away.

The blond slinks into the shadows. The Indian and the waiter are now waving their cocks in my face, begging for my services. I wolf down the waiter's, sucking him hungrily—*desperately*. My dick throbs painfully in my jeans; my precum has soaked through the thin denim. The quicker I give the waiter and the Indian their release, the quicker I get mine.

The Indian's cock swats the waiter's, and I make room for it in my mouth, sucking on both simultaneously. The two men say something, but my slurping drowns them out. Even the sound of thunder is faint.

A strangled exclamation—"Oh, god!"—cuts through the din. It's the waiter. I spit out his cock, and my hand takes over for my mouth, pumping. In seconds hot jizz splashes the corner of my mouth. The waiter's load isn't as copious as the others; after two forceful spurts his cock is dribbling. I lick his dick's dripping head, eliciting a loud grunt from the trembling young man.

The Indian butts in, roughly grabbing the top of my head and turning me toward his quivering dong. He yanks a handful of my hair and jerks my head back, making me wince in pain. I'm so turned on I'm squirming. The Indian jacks off furiously. I hear his rushed breath hissing between his clenched teeth.

"C'mon," I whisper, "give it to me."

He does. Aiming his cock at my mouth, he fires his load onto my lips, onto the tip of my nose. I open wide for more, catching his thick cream on my tongue.

Squeezing the last few drops of cum onto my lips, the Indian steps backward. His eyes are glassy, his expression dazed, like he's just awakened and can't figure out how he got here.

Shel steps into the Indian's place. He's grinning as he studies my jism-streaked face. His hard-on pushes at the front of his gray pants. I lick my lips, tasting the remnants of the strangers.

Shel likes to make me wait for it. He made me wait when he

intruded on Aaron and me those many months ago, when he made it clear I was intruding on Aaron and *him*. And he kept me waiting. I continued seeing Aaron, meeting him at Shel's high-rise apartment. Shel would be there, of course, sitting on the sidelines as I fucked Aaron. When Shel finally joined in he gave his attention—and his cock—to Aaron. Then I showed up one night and Aaron was out of the picture. Shel undressed, slowly, while I knelt at his feet, my cock hard and vibrating as I waited to satisfy this man I'd flippantly dismissed at our first meeting. Once naked, Shel still wouldn't allow me to touch his magnificent cock. Not without making me beg first.

In the alley behind the restaurant Shel unzips his pants. He's as horny as I am: his dick quivers, precum beads on the swollen cockhead. "How bad do you want it?"

"So bad my cock's about to explode."

"That's all?"

"I'd suck a hundred dicks just to get to yours."

Shel chuckles. "Only ninety-six to go."

"I'd... I'd drink their piss if you'd let me eat your cum."

His cock jumps. Shel moves closer, until his hard-on is directly over my face. A sticky thread of precum touches down on the bridge of my nose, and then Shel's dick presses against my cheek.

"You're a mess," he says, the head of his cock dabbing a gob of cum. Shel moves his dripping dong to my mouth, the creamy head nudging my trembling lips. "I should give you a shower."

I moan at the prospect, closing my eyes and opening wide. "Yes, yes," I whisper, anticipating his deluge.

But Shel pulls away.

"Stand up," he orders. I do, and he marches me across the alley to a chain-link fence. Things take a violent turn when I'm pushed against it so hard it rattles all the way to either end of the alley. I cling to the fence, looking across the garbage-strewn vacant lot as Shel, behind me, caresses my butt. He finds that hole worn in the fabric, and his fingertips brush against the crack of my ass. My sphincter contracts; my cock throbs.

Suddenly, viciously, Shel rips open my jeans, exposing my ass to the night air. Moments later a spit-lubed finger works its way between my asscheeks and into my hole. I moan loudly as his finger burrows into my chute. When that finger finds my prostate I scream. "Fuck me," I blubber.

Instead I get another finger, two digits inside my ass making me shiver. I don't know if I can take much more....

Shel withdraws his fingers briefly, and when they return to my asshole they are covered with lube. Shel always carries condoms and a small tube of lubricant, ready to fuck me whenever and wherever.

Seconds later Shel's cock replaces his fingers. No matter how many times I'm rammed by that monster, it's always a shock when Shel plunges it in. I cry out as my asslips stretch around his huge cock and his rod fills my chute. By the time his dick is buried up to the hilt, when I feel his pubic hair brushing against the skin of my butt, I'm hanging off the fence like a limp dishrag, sobbing.

Lightning flashes, thunder cracks and finally the rain comes, falling in sporadic, heavy drops.

Obscenities fall from Shel's mouth as he fucks me in hard, sharp thrusts, pushing my face against the chain-link each time he sinks his cock into my ass. Still, I beg him to fuck me harder.

For an instant I wonder if the Indian is still hanging around, watching. Then I feel Shel's weight against my back, feel his hot breath in my ear as he snarls something filthy, and no one else exists.

The ass-pounding slows as Shel reaches around my waist and fumbles with the top button of my jeans. I reach down to help him. Together we free my aching prick. When Shel touches my hard-on I almost shoot.

"Jack off into my hand," Shel says, cupping it beneath my engorged cockhead.

I'm shooting my load in less than five strokes. I'm howling ecstatically while Shel coos in my ear, "That's it, baby, give it to Daddy."

And then "Daddy" gives it to me. My body is still wracked in orgasmic throes when Shel raises the handful of cum to my face and feeds it to me. "Every drop," he hisses, and I lap up my own load.

The fucking resumes in earnest, Shel grunting with each deep thrust till, with a brutal roar, he announces he's coming.

I'm suddenly aware that it's raining harder, but I don't care. Shel pulls out of my hole and spins me around. His eyes are shining with emotion, though I can't tell if he's crying, or if it's just the rain streaming down his face. Shel seizes me in a hug so tight I think we might meld into a single being. Our cocks are crushed together between our bodies.

Shel kisses me: deep, passionate and hard. He pulls his lips away. His eyes bore into me.

"Say it," he whispers.

"I... I love you," I whimper.

The sick part is I do. I really do.

CLOSET CASE

Martin Delacroix

Call me a jerk, but I have a problem with closeted guys, these so-called "bi-curious" men. Deep inside most are gay, I believe, but they're scared to admit it. So they lead the straight life, looking down on us poor faggots. When the urge strikes they'll sneak off and slum with the queers, but an hour later they're back with the wife and the kids, safe and happy.

What bullshit.

I fell for such a guy once; his name was Kenneth. He'd tell his wife he was going to a sports bar with his buds, then he'd come to my place and I'd fuck his ass into next week. The more we did it the more I craved him, and one night, while we lay in bed, I begged him to quit his marriage. I cried, even. I said I loved him, that we were meant to be together, but he said no, it wasn't possible, and after that I never saw him again. The bastard dumped me, leaving me so depressed I nearly jumped off a bridge.

That was a year ago, and up until last week I still wasn't over it; I continued to suffer.

Then something happened.

Last Saturday afternoon I occupied a stool at the Rocket Club, a gay club in our town. I was speaking with the bartender, Gordon, when this guy strolled in, someone I'd never seen in the place before. He wore a T-shirt, a ball cap and a pair of blue jeans riding low so you could see the waistband of his briefs. He ordered a glass of beer, then he tapped his wedding band against the edge of the bar, keeping time with a song that played on the jukebox.

There were maybe a dozen guys in the Rocket, and this fellow's gaze moved from face to face till it came to mine and our eyes met. He dipped his chin and I nodded back, and once he got his beer he approached, extending his hand.

He said, "Hi, I'm Danny." His voice was pretty deep and he spoke with an accent. (Alabama?) I told him I was Ian and we shook hands, then he took a stool next to mine, facing me so our knees touched.

He looked twenty-five, maybe, half a head shorter than me, slim with a bit of muscle. His hair was wavy and fawn-colored, and it grew over his ears. He was fair skinned and freckles danced across his nose like confetti, giving him a boyish look. His eyes were the color of Gulf water—between green and blue. His teeth were large, as white as piano keys.

We made small talk.

I told him I was a drywall hanger by trade, but I'd been laid off, and right now I worked the counter at a bait and tackle shop. "It doesn't pay well," I said, "so I'm looking around."

He was a housepainter, he said. It didn't pay well either.

I asked about the ring on his finger.

"I'm married. Got a little girl, age three."

I must've looked at him funny 'cause he said, "I'm not gay; I just need a man's touch now and then."

I said, "I guess this is one of those times?"

He looked at me and winked, and anger stirred in my belly. *Goddamned closet case.*

Still, he was attractive.

He asked my age and I told him. His gaze traveled from my eyes to my boots, then back. He said, "For thirty you're in great shape."

I'm no pretty boy, but I stay fit. At six-two, I keep my weight around one-ninety. My hair is buzzed and my chin's stubbled, and I've got tattoos on both forearms. Guys who like their men butch are attracted to me.

My sexual tastes?

I'm a total top, and while I wouldn't call myself a pervert, I like a little kink. I can get rough, too, when I'm in the mood.

I asked Danny how often he strayed and he said, "Every few months, maybe."

I shifted position on my stool, moving closer to him, my knee rubbing his inner thigh. I looked at him and flickered my eyebrows, and this caused his cheeks to color. He glanced into his lap, then he raised his chin and his gaze met mine.

He said, "Do you like me?"

I nodded.

He pointed his chin at the door. "Well?"

I said, "Sure, why not?"

We don't have basements in Florida—the water table's too high—but one room in my house I've converted to sort of a sex chamber. It's soundproofed and the windows are blacked out. There's a bed, of course, and a padded bench. A metal frame, nine feet high with an adjustable crossbar, is anchored to the floor; it faces a mirrored wall. I have spotlights on the ceiling with dimmer switches, a lantern with a red lens and a black light as well. I can alter the atmosphere to suit any occasion. A footlocker holds toys: cuffs and dildos of varying sizes and shapes, instruments of discipline, cock rings and butt plugs and so forth.

Danny studied the trunk's contents, arms crossed at his chest, weight resting upon one leg. The ceiling lights were on and they reflected in his hair and eyes. He licked one corner of his mouth with the tip of his tongue. He said, "I'm sure you'll think I'm boring. I've never, you know…"

"What?"

"Done more than get blown."

"You're kidding?"

He shook his head, shoving his hands into his front pockets and studying his shoes.

I came to him and crooked an arm around his neck, pulling his chest to mine. I kissed his neck, just beneath the jawline, then I ground my stubble against his smooth cheek. His breathing accelerated and I felt his heart thump in his chest. I whispered, "You can do anything you like in this room. What happens here is our secret."

He said, "Okay."

When I moved my mouth to his, he turned his face.

"What's wrong?" I said.

"I don't kiss—not guys anyway."

"Why?"

He turned his face toward mine, and his eyes narrowed. "I told you, I'm not gay."

I lowered my gaze, thinking, *Sure, pal.* Then I looked him in the eye. "When you jack off, do you sometimes think about men?"

His cheeks reddened and he glanced away. "Once in a while."

"Describe your fantasies. What happens?"

He smirked. "Why? Are you a psychologist?"

"Just curious," I said. "You're uncomfortable right now, aren't you?"

He dropped the smirk and nodded.

"Why?"

"I told you already, I don't do this often. Guys suck me off in their car and that's about it."

"But you've thought about doing more?"

"Yeah, of course."

The only sound in the room was cool air flowing from a ceiling register. My thermostat was set at seventy-four degrees, but Danny's T-shirt was dark in the armpits and I seized it by the hem. "Let me take this off you."

Our eyes met and he blinked two or three times. "All right," he said.

He raised his hands and I lifted the shirt from his torso, yanking it over his head. His chest was smooth and defined, with quarter-sized areolas and nipples like match heads. His shoulders and biceps were underdeveloped, but his belly was flat and his abdominal muscles rippled under the skin.

He said, "Take your shirt off, too."

And I said, "Why don't you do it for me?"

His hands shook when he did so. Once I was bare chested I pulled him to me so our hipbones met. I nuzzled his ear with the tip of my nose. His chin rested upon my shoulder, and I smelled his hair and it reminded me of fresh straw. His erection nudged my groin.

"Tell me," I said, "what you'd like to do."

He swallowed and didn't answer.

I reached for his buttcheek and squeezed. "Come on, say."

He exhaled, shifting his weight. "Sometimes my wife...ties me up."

I thought, *Hmmm. That's better.* Then I said, "You're naked when she does this?"

"Yep."

"What else does she do? After you're restrained?"

"Different stuff."

"Like?"

He giggled nervously, shaking his head. "This is embarrassing."

"It's okay. Go on."

His cock was rigid as a broomstick. He kept shifting his weight as he spoke—it was almost like we were slow dancing. "She spanks my ass. She pinches my nuts and my cock, my nipples too."

"And you like that?"

He nodded.

Go ahead, ask him.

I said, "Do you feel like doing that now?"

He didn't answer.

I placed a hand at the small of his back, hooking a thumb inside the waistband of his jeans. "Giving up control can be sexy. You have to trust is all."

Danny didn't respond. He kept rocking, hips pressed against mine.

I said, "Surrendering your freedom is a first step."

He froze, then. Lifting his chin from my shoulder, he took a step backward, looking at me with his forehead crinkled. "You want to tie me up?"

I shrugged. "Something like that."

He rubbed the tip of his nose and stared at the floor. "I don't know..."

I went to the footlocker and produced a pair of leather cuffs, the adjustable kind, fitted with spring-loaded clips. Handing one to Danny, I pointed to the metal frame. "I can hook you up and we'll have some fun."

Danny studied the frame, the mirrored wall, then the cuff, his jaw working from side to side. His erection was visible in his pants, jutting down one leg. He raised his chin and his gaze met mine. "You mentioned trust..."

I nodded.

"We hardly know each other. How do I know you're not some sort of freak?"

"You know where I live; you saw the truck I drive. I'm a working stiff, yeah, but I'm not a drifter or an ex-con." I looked into Danny's face. "You're safe with me."

He swallowed, keeping his gaze level with mine. "If I say quit something, you've got to stop. Understand?"

"Of course."

"I'm not bullshitting."

"Neither am I." I'm *such* a liar.

Danny moistened his lips, staring at the cuff in his hand. Then he raised his chin and looked at me.

"All right," he said. "Let's do it."

I brought him bottled water and he drank a pint or so. At my request, he removed his shoes and socks. I sat on the padded bench and he stood before me, his chest rising and falling while I slipped the cuffs onto his wrists, adjusting the buckles till they fit tight. The black leather looked sexy on Danny, contrasting with his fair skin.

I took him by his forearm and led him to the frame. The spotlights on the ceiling cast intense beams, made his eyes sparkle. Standing between the frame's vertical bars, he faced the mirrored wall, hands raised above his head, displaying sandy-colored hair in his armpits. I adjusted the crossbar, locking it into place at a height just under nine feet. Danny kept his gaze on the mirror before him, flexing his toes while I clipped each cuff to the bar, immobilizing him. His arms were fully extended and his hands were spread apart so they hung directly above his shoulders. He stood flat-footed, but barely, as I hadn't left him much play. He could twist at the waist or hop up and down, but that was all.

From the closet I produced a digital movie camera and a tripod and as soon as Danny saw them he protested. "I didn't agree to filming."

I shrugged and set things up, focusing the lens on Danny. I stood on a chair and adjusted the ceiling fixtures so he was properly lit.

He said, "Did you hear me? Don't turn that thing on."

I ignored his remark and did exactly that. Then I stepped behind him, pressing my hips to his buttocks, wrapping my arms about his waist and squeezing. In the mirror, my face was visible over his shoulder, and I rubbed his cheek with my stubble. I said, "You look good strung up."

His chest rose and fell and his breath whistled in his nose. He said, "I don't like this; turn me loose."

I slapped the back of his head, making him flinch. I said, "You're staying put, my friend."

That shut him up.

I popped open the button at the waistband of his jeans, my thumb knuckle digging into his belly. I asked, "Has a man ever stripped you?"

He shook his head, wrenching his lips.

I lowered his zipper and parted his pant flaps, exposing char-coal-colored briefs. "It's a bit freaky the first time, losing your britches to a guy you barely know."

My cock had stiffened; it pressed against his behind and his buttocks clenched. I backed up a step and shucked his jeans down to his ankles. His thighs were smooth, his calves freckled and dusted with hair the same color as that in his armpits. I told him to step out of his pants and he did, but it took some effort—several kicks, in fact—before they finally came off. It was like his body didn't want to surrender them.

Again, I pressed my hips to his buttocks and rested my chin on his shoulder. I wrapped my arms about his chest and squeezed, forcing air from his lungs. His cock was rigid and thick as a cucumber. It throbbed against the flimsy fabric of his briefs.

I slipped my index finger inside the waistband. "Let's get rid of these."

He drew a breath, shifting his weight and staring at his reflection while sweat trickled from his armpits.

I snatched the undershorts to midthigh, exposing his genitals. His cock bobbed before him and his testicles dangled in their shaved sac. His pubic hair was trimmed to a small patch, and just behind his cockhead, on the underside of the shaft, a gold post glistened. Teasing it with a fingernail, I said, "What's this?"

"My wife's idea. She likes the way it feels inside her."

"Did it hurt when they installed it?"

He nodded.

"But you did as she asked?"

"I did as I was *told*."

I chuckled. *Good answer.*

I peeled the briefs to his ankles and he kicked them aside. His asscheeks were like two cantaloupes, smooth and white as porcelain, firm to the touch. I slapped one buttock and the sound of the swat echoed in the room.

I said, "If you're smart, you'll do what I say too."

He flexed his toes and didn't speak.

A willow switch is a fine corporal punishment tool. It stings like hell, imparting wicked stripes, but it doesn't make much noise, nor does it break skin if properly applied. I'm handy with one, and now I introduced Danny to my technique, a series of strokes delivered with an inconsistent tempo, tormenting his buttocks and the backs of his thighs. I got him dancing in short order, yelping and twisting about, and after a half-dozen blows he shouted, "That's enough. Quit."

I responded by switching his thighs anew, several strokes in quick succession. The assault produced threats and curses, in between yelps: "When I get loose I'm gonna—*ouch*—kick your ass." And "*Ouch.* I'll kill you, motherfucker." And "You're dead meat, you...*Jesus* that hurts."

I told myself: *This pussy couldn't kick his grandma's butt, much less mine.*

Now, a guy in Danny's position must cross a certain threshold. He has to learn that, despite any prerestraint assurances to the contrary, he's lost control of his situation. I didn't dignify his threats with a verbal response. Instead, I kept on switching, giving him another dozen strokes, raising more angry welts on his ass and thighs, bringing forth shrieks and wails. By the time I ceased, Danny had lost control of his bladder and pissed all over the floor. He sweated buckets and pled for mercy. ("I swear I'll do anything you want—*anything*.")

Whipping him was fun—I could have continued for hours—but I didn't want to kill the guy. I just wanted him to know I considered him a punk, a closeted weasel.

I sat on the padded bench, placing the switch beside me, and I drank bottled water, studying Danny's visage. His face was crimson and distorted and ceiling lights reflected off his skin. He sniffled while his eyes flitted between mine and the switch, no doubt wondering if I planned to whip him further.

"Having fun?" I asked.

He shook his head like a panicky child.

I approached and seized his nipple between my thumb and index finger, using my nails, pinching and twisting, making Danny squirm. I changed nipples, pinching and twisting some more, and went back and forth while Danny whimpered. He said, "Please, don't," but I kept on till both tits were purple and swollen.

His penis had gone soft during the switching, but now it stiffened, ticking upward till it pointed at the ceiling. I fetched a leather cock ring, the kind with snaps, and slipped it beneath his scrotum then secured it to the base of his cock so his nuts bulged and his erection wouldn't subside. I flicked at his boner, making it jiggle. I pinched his sac and listened to him suck air through clenched teeth.

Okay, I'll admit I enjoyed doing these things to Mr. Closet Case. His chest heaved and he trembled. He flinched each time I touched him, as if my fingers delivered electric shocks to his body. His armpits smelled funky and their scent got me horny. I licked them nice and slow, savoring their salty taste, using my teeth to tug at his spit-soaked hairs.

Danny whimpered. He said, "Stop, please. Let me go."

I lifted my face from his armpit and frowned. Seizing the switch, I whipped his buttocks again, a series of ten strokes that drove him into a frenzy, making him howl and bounce his heels. His ass looked like he'd sat on a hot barbeque grill, more than once. When I'd finished I stood before him and took his chin in my hand, forcing him to look at me. His breath huffed and sweat coated his forehead. Fresh tears leaked from his pretty eyes. I said, "I'll release you when I'm ready, not until. Understand?"

He nodded, blinking more tears.

"Now, let's talk about sex," I said.

He dropped his gaze.

I said, "I'm a faggot and I'll bet you are too."

"I told you, I'm married, I've never—"

"Don't feed me your bullshit. The sooner you admit you're gay, the quicker we'll be finished here."

I toyed with Danny's nuts, rolling them around in my hand.

"Is that what you want to hear?" he said. "That I'm gay?"

"More than that."

"What?"

"Ask me to fuck your faggot ass."

He hung his head, but I chucked his chin with a knuckle and made him look at me.

"Go on," I said, "ask."

When he didn't speak, I seized the willow switch, but before I could use it Danny started babbling. "Okay, all right; I'll say whatever you want"

I tapped the switch against the palm of my hand. "I'm waiting."

He closed his eyes. "I'm queer," he said. "I've always been."

"Then how come you're married?"

He looked at me then dropped his gaze. "I'm a chicken shit, that's why."

"Ever been butt-fucked?"

"No."

"So, this will be your first time?"

He nodded.

"Go ahead, now: ask me."

He swallowed and his voice shook when he spoke. "I want you to fuck me."

"You want me to fuck *what*?"

He lowered his chin. "My...faggot ass."

Okay, Ian, that's enough. End this.

Exhaling, I removed the cock ring from Danny's genitals. Then, stepping behind him, I released his cuffs from the crossbar, one at a time, opening the clips. His arms fell to his sides, and he sank to his knees, into a puddle of his own piss. He looked up at me with his eyebrows arched and his forehead furrowed.

"What are you doing?" he asked.

"Letting you loose," I said.

I pointed to his clothes. "Go ahead, get dressed and leave."

A vertical crease appeared between his eyebrows, then he dropped his gaze and he did not move.

I said, "Hold up your hands and I'll remove the cuffs."

He did so and I took them off and then I placed them in the footlocker. When I turned back toward Danny, he still had not budged. He looked up at me and said, "I don't understand."

"We're done here. Go home to your wife."

He moistened his lips. "I don't have a wife," he said.

"Huh?"

"I was lying. It's a thing I do sometimes, when I'm in a strange town. I pretend to be someone I'm not."

Oh, shit.

I sat on the bench and rubbed my face with my hands. Then I looked at Danny. "So, who are you, really?"

He blew air out his nose and shook his head. "Just another faggot—in this case a queer with a whipped ass." He glanced over his shoulder and looked at his reflection in the mirrored wall. "You tore me up."

"I'm sorry," I said. "I've got this thing about closeted guys; I was angry and—"

He held up a hand. "It's okay, I deserved it."

I shrugged.

"Plus," he said, looking at me and crinkling the corners of his eyes, "it *was* awfully sexy."

I started at his remark. Then I chuckled and shook my head. I said, "Here I thought I was in control..."

He smiled, raising a shoulder then letting it drop, and looked away.

I said, "You want to clean yourself up?"

He rose to his feet. "Maybe later. Right now I was hoping we'd, you know…"

"What?"

"Finish what we started."

Go ahead, Ian. After the thrashing he took, he's earned it.

I took him on his back, on the bed, my hips slapping his whipped buttocks each time I thrust. His hole was tight; it flexed against the shaft of my cock and felt delicious. Danny allowed me to kiss him now. He sucked my tongue while we fucked, while I pinched his tortured nipples and ran my hands over the welts on his thighs and ass. When I came inside him he shot his load right away, scattering sticky pearls across his chest and belly.

"That was nice," he whispered.

Thirty minutes later, after a shower, he was gone. I never even found out his real name.

But here's the funny part: after he left in his pickup truck I stood on my front porch, watching his taillights fade, and, I swear, I felt as though a weight had lifted from my shoulders. For the first time in a year, I didn't feel bad about getting dumped by Kenneth. In fact, I was glad he wasn't in my life any longer, the creep.

I went back inside and found a bucket and a mop and a bottle of sudsy ammonia, then I cleaned up the puddle of piss my guest had left me. He'd offered to do it himself, of course, but I told him no, I'd take care of things.

It was the least I could do to thank him.

A NOSE COMMITS SUICIDE

Daniel Allen Cox

It's a horrible substance to drown in, given my affinity for it. But after you read this, I think you'll understand why I performed the final, fatal inhalation. Technically, it's called "natricide"—death by violence to the nostrils—but I call it madness.

I did it for his body.

He would toss his hair, pretending to clear it from his eyes. I knew, however, that it was really to tease me closer with an explosion of oils, to seduce me with sebum. In the summer heat, his glands oozed everything I liked.

Then he'd tip his hair with gel and toss a little more, wafting chemicals my way and ruining the moment. I'd skulk off. Of course, he was hurt by my disdain for hair products, but kept tossing for other noses to hide his pain.

I was deceitful, too. When he wasn't looking, I'd position myself downwind and sniff. I couldn't get enough.

* * *

Betcha my family photo album looks nothing like yours.

Close-up of me as a baby nose: swaddled in blankets and my own newborn smell. My pores—which would later become thick marshes of blackheads—were still closed. I'm a shiny button, yet to be awakened by the rot and bloom of life. Oh, wait—there's a wrinkle. Perhaps an awareness that breast milk was only a few feet away...

Another shot, one of my favorites: a curious honker, growing but still little. Far too hungry for sugar. Jolly Rancher is a square candy. Nostrils are round. Tell me this blockage isn't the most amazing thing you've ever seen.

You might say that it was obvious, even way back then, that I was headed for trouble.

I'd swarm him as soon as he took off his socks. I found a fresh day's mold irresistible, especially when packaged in new-shoe smell. The most precious substances on earth are matured: Oka cheese, 1983 Chateau Lafite Rothschild, toe funk. I loved watching NBA basketball, because I knew that the players all harbored the same beautiful problem.

His balls were a swamp where I went to get lost: scrotum so rich in folds, trapping his every secretion and distilling it into deliciousness. Piss drops would evaporate there, leaving salty rings that smelled like the semen hidden inside him, a tang like bleach. The scent of his pisshole changed with his diet: tuna, maple syrup, coffee, apples.

Lime Jell-O was a dead giveaway.

Know that I didn't kill myself over a boy. His smells were so much better than he was.

The phone rang during one of our sniff sessions, and I let it go to voice mail. Later, when I checked my messages, I heard my doctor saying she wanted to discuss "some of her findings." I put off calling her back, because it didn't sound like a dermatology issue. It sounded like something I didn't want to hear.

This one's a Polaroid. Puberty had finally given me a bit of heft, puffed me out with pride. In the shot, I'm sprouting pubes in both nostrils. With my blackheads and acne, I was engaged in all-out war with the world. My fighting stance was angular and defined, because the sun hit from the side and cast half of me in shadow, like it does with the Great Pyramids at sundown.

You'll have to forgive me for having a superiority complex. It's just that the Egyptians built the pyramids in the shape of noses, and it's all rather flattering...

His bike gave me months of pleasure at a time. After a sweaty, summer ride through the city, he'd strip and sink into a chair in front of the TV. A smile would creep across his face as I planted myself between his splayed legs and sniffed his nuts and perineum until I passed out from the concentrated virility. Like breathing pure, scented oxygen. His ass was equally intoxicating.

Pits are nice, but too vanilla. I've always made a point of exploring the uncharted body. The waist and wrist often smell like rubber (underwear elastic, waterproof Casio). Behind the knee can be buttery, and shins can be pine fresh.

We are all synaesthetes but with different wiring. That is to say, our senses are connected in ways we might never understand. For you, the smell of grass burning in the sun will make you feel the snakebite all over again. BBQ chicken will always sound like Radiohead.

For me—a nose—it's the opposite. All stimuli lead to smell, and that's why I'm no longer with you.

One day, the shit hit the fan. This is no cliché, because I could actually smell the feces radiating down as it spun around on the fan blades.

I finally went to see my doctor.

"Chemosensory disturbance," she said.

"What are you talking about."

"You have smell impairment, and it's getting worse."

"Impossible! I could smell you from outside," I said.

"Dysosmia. The smells are distorted. You're already relying on memory, because you're not smelling much."

"You're such a fucking odor-kill. I hate you."

"I'm sorry," she said, "but there are ways to cope with this."

At first, I didn't think it was that bad. The nose is a memory cum-dump; I was a hard drive with forty gigs of RAM that archived every whiff, scent, waft and hint I'd ever detected. I had interpreted this man as a mindmap of smells and could conjure a Smell-O-Vision rendering of him anytime I pleased.

The memories were perfect. But that was exactly the problem. They were sterile.

His hair smelled like Pantene Pro-V, even when he hadn't taken a shower in days, his feet like laundry lint and fabric softener. Crotch? Bicycle seat and Irish Spring soap. My memory had frozen out any trace of raunch. In other words, pure fucking hell.

I was guaranteed a lifetime of smells not worth smelling.

What follows is the text from the back of a box of Lime Jell-O. I hope, for your sake, that you never have to follow these instructions:

Add mix to 1 cup boiling water, stir until dissolved.
Add 2 cups ice-cold water, refrigerate until it sets.
Dive in.

* * *

A final photo. I'm sealed in green gelatin, entombed with my too-perfect memories the way pharaohs were buried with their treasures and gems. The Jell-O is in the shape of the Great Pyramid of Giza, replica limestone bricks jagged and crumbling where I jumped in. As limey as lime gets.

What stinks is that when I inhaled for the last time, I couldn't taste a damn thing.

THE LAST PICTURE. SHOW.

James Earl Hardy

BuTay had had enough.

You can't fake the fuck, a nut is a must—especially if you're doin' it on camera. If the one you're with isn't bringing out the freak in you, you gotta do whatever and think about *whoever* to bring it. Don't let up that you've been let down. Keep a, *ahem*, straight face and make the camera believe you. 'Cause the camera never lies.

It's not the first time he's had to put on a fuckin' happy face (or is that a happy fuckin' face?), but it will be the last. This is it for him. *This is it.* His last picture. Yes, he's said it before and he's meant it before, but this time the decision has been made for him.

This Big D. You guessed it, aka Big Dick. With a name like that if he wasn't doing porn he'd be a pimp, a rapper or some combination thereof (they are more often than not all-in-one

THE LAST PICTURE. SHOW.

these days). He's a walking caricature. An obnoxious rope-a-dope chain swinging from his neck, diamond studs in each ear, silver rings on his right fingers, gold on his left (including the thumbs) and a grill that caps his upper row. Dipped in ink on his right thigh (something in Chinese), his left arm (something in Japanese), his spine (a scorpion) and above his navel (an arrow pointing downward with DA SHYT tattooed above it). And the splotchy mark just below his right shoulder blade? Apparently the result of a drive-by in Compton, where he filled his gangsta scorecard as a drug dealer.

The main attractions are the brick-house bod, that big ol' dick (a ruler by six and three-quarter inches), and the sac (dubbed "Monster's Balls"). Ever since he exploded (pun intended) on the scene a couple of years ago, he's been the talk. The public can't get enough of him.

BuTay thought he wouldn't be able to get enough of him too. The man is *f-f-f-fine* and, from what he could tell, knew how to throw it down. And BuTay felt rather honored: he would be the first man Big would do onscreen (the jury is still out on whether he has done it off). Several studios—such as FreakDawg and PitBull—tried to woo him, but he said yes to Full Moons and its president/director/producer, Ernest Jamison aka EJ, because EJ could promise him the person...no, the *ass* he's always wanted to nail.

But whatever excitement BuTay felt disintegrated when they met.

BuTay has three "hell-2-the-naw" commandments: no drugs, no bareback and no raining on his face. And in a world where the three often go hand in hand, that he's been able to avoid them all is something of a miracle.

So it's a rather poetic form of justice that he would be faced with all three today.

When they were in the "dressing/makeup room" (a large walk-in utility closet), Big decided to light up a joint. "Wanna puff?"

Not, "Do you mind if I smoke?" But, at least he offered. He has manners.... "No thanks."

"Mo' fo' me, then."

Good thing he's one of those artists who frowns on intimacy (i.e., kissing, hugging, cuddling); BuTay wouldn't have to inhale the stank on his lips.

As they rehearsed—choreographing their movements so that they'd always be on camera and on cue—Big had the audacity to ask, "You mind if we do this raw, dawg?" He'd done it bareback with women.

But not with BuTay. "Yes I do."

"You ain't gotta worry. I got me."

Yeah, you got you; who's gonna have me?

He kept pleading his case. "Ain't no problem. I can pull out befo' I blow."

"You won't be pullin' in if you're not covered."

He shrugged. "A'ight, a'ight, son. No prob."

Uh-huh. I know it won't be.

And after almost a half hour of some very uninspired pumpin' and pushin', it seemed as if he was about to blow—and would no doubt be springing forth his seed on BuTay's face. It was bad enough BuTay had to listen to this motherfucker have sex with *himself...*

"This shit is hot, ain't it?"

"No doubt, money."

"I'm committin' a genocide on this azz, huh?"

"You sho' is, dawg."

Yawn.

...and that he couldn't keep his shit up. Twice during the fuck scene BuTay had to go down on him.

He wasn't about to let Big use his face as a towel. If BuTay wanted a facial, he'd go to a spa.

And it was obvious that, despite BuTay's protests, EJ was fine with letting it happen. And why wouldn't he be: Big is an executive producer on *Big's Big Break*, a credit that EJ had always denied BuTay despite his being his biggest star and making over a million dollars for him in two years. This bit of information was revealed by Big minutes before the shoot began—and you know that left a *very* bitter taste in BuTay's mouth. When confronted, EJ at first denied it but then dismissed it as "just business." Uh-huh. And the expression he wore as Big ejected his dick and went for the condom broadcasted the same sentiment.

It was in that moment that BuTay's whole career flashed before his eyes. His bootay had seen better days. *Much* better days.

BuTay—or Evan, as his parents named him—didn't fall into the biz because he was trying to feed a drug habit. Or needed a warm bed to sleep in for a night or two. He wasn't molested or sexually abused as a child and was exorcising those demons by playing with himself and others in public. Nor was he hard up for money. Or hard up.

He answered an ad in *HX Magazine*—to be an office manager. He was a junior at NYU pursuing a degree in creative writing (a career choice that disappointed his parents). He had never managed an office but the work hours fell on days he wasn't in class and the position didn't require experience. The ad stated: "Charismatic cutie with bootie needed to oversee clerical operations, Thurs-Sat, 1pm–9pm."

Charismatic cutie with bootie. That was him.

He got the job because he was the only Negro out of the dozen candidates that applied. That's what EJ wanted all along, but he couldn't very well include that in the ad. Why any of the

white boys showed up was a mystery: even a porn outsider like
Evan was aware of EJ's predilection for dark meat.

Which is why Evan wore his tightest pair of jeans to the
"interview." One look was all it took: after dismissing all the
vanilla, they sat in a corner of the Lower East Side loft that also
functioned as EJ's office, where he made one offer Evan couldn't
refuse—and another that he could.

After agreeing on his pay and going over his duties, EJ walked
him out, zeroing in on his backside. "You oughta be in pictures
with an ass like that."

BuTay figured that most Black men he laid that line on were
appreciative. Not him. "I don't think so."

EJ was thrown by the response. "You don't think so? Why
not?"

Why not. As in, *Why wouldn't you want to be in pictures,
since I, the white man, said you would be good in them, I know
everything, and I know what's best for everyone, including
you.*

"Because I know what's best for me and that's not it."

"Well...have you ever been photographed nude? You might
change your mind once you see how beautiful you are."

Beautiful. BuTay had heard that from many a white man
eager to get into his pants. "Don't you mean how beautiful my
ass is?"

"Uh, well, yeah," he admitted with nervous laughter.

"I'll be keeping my clothes on."

He kept that promise—for a year. EJ continued his quest to
convince Evan to act (suggesting that he ease into the biz by
doing a solo scene with a dildo) and become his lover (need-
lessly patting his ass as if they were on a basketball team and
brushing behind him *very* slowly). And many of the actors who
came through Full Moons' doors really tempted him to take off

his clothes, on and off camera. The boiz—Black, Latino and Bla-tino—were too fuckin' fine for words; most flirted with him, some pushed up (literally), and a few requested, with dick in hand, that he "fluff" them before they went on camera. It also didn't help that EJ sometimes filmed in the upstairs bunker; the sounds and smells were hard to ignore—and made *him* hard. But he resisted and never saw anyone outside the office; he didn't want to get a reputation for sleeping with his employer's actors. He knew that if he took just one baby step in that direction, he would be pulled all the way in.

It's just a matter of time, many told him, *before you take that dive*. Unfortunately for EJ, it didn't happen in a film he directed. It was on a Monday before class, and Evan dropped by the office to pick up his paycheck. EJ was helping cast *Ruffnecks & Rednecks*; he and Jess Cunningham, the president of Good Ol' Boy Productions and the director/producer/writer of *R & R* (yeah, believe it or not, porn flicks *do* have scripts, even if they aren't longer than a dozen pages), had seen fifty actors over two days and no one had captured Jess's eye.

But when Jess saw Evan walk in the door, the search was over.

"Well, it's about time!" Jess cried like Anthony Perkins after he first lays eyes on Diana Ross in *Mahogany*. He swooped down on BuTay like a vulture and ushered him over to a couch where one of the proposed rednecks, an Oliver Platt look-alike wearing black jeans and a white muscle tee, sat.

"He's not here to audition," EJ dryly stated. Evan frowned at him. *That's right, white man, speak for me like you always know you can.*

"Are you kidding me? He's *perfect*." He turned to Evan. *"You* are Benji."

EJ did the introductions (the "redneck" in question going by the name Peeter Paul), after which Evan politely informed him, "I'm not an actor."

"With *that* face? *That* body?" Jess's eyes dropped down. "And *that* junky trunk?"

Oh, no. Another wannabe-hip white boy in our midst. At least EJ didn't pretend to be down or get it; he left the Blackisms to the ones who know and do them the best.

"*You* are Benji," he repeated, just in case it was missed the first time.

Evan didn't have the chance to respond—Jess handed him a copy of the script and pointed to the description of Benjamin, aka Benji, highlighted in orange: Black as midnight, very thick full lips, light lust-filled eyes, short haircut, medium muscular build, ass like a donkey.

It was borderline racist. Yet... *That's me*, Evan thought to himself.

"*You* are the man I have always dreamed of bringing this character to life. Please, *please* read for me," Jess pleaded.

Evan glanced at EJ, who shrugged.

"Hey, Boss, can you give me a lift?" As Evan read the line, Peeter Paul's eyes were glued to Evan's ass.

"Uh..." Jess began, cautiously. "Can you be more... ethnic?"

"More what?"

"You know, more...more ghetto." Uh-huh. *You mean more niggerish, like the slave master said in the movie* Drum, *right?*

"I didn't grow up in a ghetto." And he didn't. Coral Springs is a way-upper-middle-class enclave twenty miles south of Detroit. Like his father (a pediatrician) and mother (an insurance adjustor), his neighbors earned close to seven figures annually, sent their children to the Jack & Jill club and to HBCU's, and vacationed on Martha's Vineyard in the summer and the

Poconos in the fall. So his vocabulary wasn't sprinkled with "yo," "ain't," and the ever-popular "nigga," even after living in Crown Heights for three years.

"Oh." Jess was clearly surprised (or was that disappointment?).

But Evan knew just what he wanted.

"I'll give it a try." He winked at EJ; EJ knew he was playing with him. Evan's posture became slumped. He put on his DON'T FUCK WITH ME mask, which he had perfected while living in da 'hood. He glared at Peeter Paul, who leaned back. His voice went from tenor to baritone, with a little scratchiness in the throat added for affect. "Ya Boss. Can ya gimme a lif'?"

Evan never thought he'd see someone do it, but Jess jumped for joy. *That's it!*

Both Evan and EJ smiled.

Jess paced, clapping furiously. "We'll fly you down to Atlanta next Wednesday. You can stay at my home. I'm sure EJ won't mind doing without you for a couple of days...."

"Sorry, but I'm not your man," Evan interrupted.

"But you *are*," he replied.

"I can't."

"Yes, you *can*."

"It's not something I want to do."

"You'll want to."

Jess ignored the *no*. He called Evan on his cell. He called him at his apartment. He emailed him. He sent flowers to the office, even a "flesh-o-gram" (a buffed brother who disrobed to a hip-hop version of "There's No Business Like Show Business"). But it was that "final, *final* offer" he put on the table (he presented him with five) that changed his mind.

* * *

Evan (now christened BuTay) wasn't looking forward to being pawed and plowed by a ratty ragamuffin named (what else?) Bubba, who looked like he just rolled out from *under* the trailer park (balding, bearded and beer-bellied), but managed not to reveal that he was totally creeped out by the fellow's clammy hands, pungent body odor, and monstrously hairy back (after all, it's called *acting*). As it turned out, once he and Bubba got into it, it was a hell of a lot better than he thought it could be: the man wasn't a bad kisser, devoured BuTay's dick like his life depended on it, had somethin' to work with himself (nine inches with a decent width), and *worked* BuTay rather nicely in four different positions (bent over, doggie, on his back and BuTay's favorite, sitting down). Add the thick humidity of a sweltering Atlanta afternoon; the incessant buzz of the gnats and mosquitoes; a rusty, rickety red and blue pickup truck; a ripped, stained mattress; BuTay chewing on Bubba's pink, fuzzy balls; Bubba gnawing on BuTay's asshole as his scruffy beard scratched BuTay's unblemished booty; the thump of the gun rack (hooked to the back window and holding an AK-47 rifle) as BuTay bumped his ass down and Bubba pumped his dick up; BuTay decorating Bubba's face (Bubba insisted) and Bubba polishing BuTay's ass with his own cream...and you had the makings of a *semen*al moment in porn, a moment that Smutmeister, the critic for the online zine Get Off, described as "one of the most repulsive *and* hottest fucking scenes ever."

Evan *was* repulsed by the whole experience, yet that was the key to making it so hot. It was nasty sex with a nasty man—and he made it even *nastier*, upping the *eeeeeeew* factor with some inspired improvisation (snacking on Bubba's crusty toes and catching the sweat dropping off his forehead with his tongue), moaning his lines with bone-chilling sureness (*"Rock me wit' dat cock, Papa Bear, yeeeaaah!"* and *"Bang ma big black bu-tay, Bubba!"*) and yodeling (it would become his celluloid hall-mark). And, any time he began to lose the lust Jess recognized in his eyes—or the breakfast he had eaten several hours before they filmed—he thought of the $10,000 cashier's check he'd receive at the end of the day's shoot.

What people do for money...

The *pre*verted passion BuTay exuded was so convincing that he earned the GayVN award (the Oscar of queer porn) for Best Supporting Actor, the first Negro victor (the voters must've forgotten he was the lead). Smutmeister christened him "the Hattie McDaniel of Gay Smut" (since Smutmeister quoted him as declaring, "I'd rather play a ho' than be one," and BuTay wore a stars and bars bandana on his head in the film, the comparison was convenient though misguided), and his triumph was heralded as "a new day for the industry." What that "new day" was supposed to look like and bring with it no one ever explained, although the implication was clear to most: Black actors had "arrived" and would receive commensurate pay, perks and promotion. Of course, that day never came, but BuTay did become the new "it" boy. He made two more *R & R* flicks, getting *very* trashy with Shane, a Toby Keith twin, in a truck stop bathroom. Their filthiest scenes: Shane splashing Coors and licking it off of BuTay's chest, back and ass; BuTay cleaning out the cheese clumped under Shane's foreskin with his tongue and Shane sticking his lit cigar into BuTay's ass—and BuTay *smoking* it. His reunion with Bubba for a barnyard frolic was almost as nauseating as their first romp: wrestling naked in a giant aluminum tub full of slop; BuTay inhaling and licking Bubba's sweaty, smelly armpits and Bubba using BuTay's bootay as the bowl and inserting a carrot, an ear of corn, a cucumber and slithers of tomato to create the ultimate garden salad. BuTay got back-to-back Best Actor GayVN nods.

After that, the make of white man selected as his costars improved *dramatically* (Black men are usually paired with white men who are, for lack of a better word, trolls), beginning with the *International BuTay* series, which chronicled his sexploits with men of different European backgrounds (Russian, French, Spanish and British) during a gymnastics competition (BuTay got pummeled on the pommel horse); a Foreign Legion boot camp (the four soldiers had a ball declaring war on his ass); a soccer match (the Madrid boys had thighs—and dicks—of steel, and BuTay thoroughly enjoyed squeezing and pleasing them all) and a rehearsal for an all-male production of *Hamlet* (the tagline: "Ay, *He's* the Rub!").

In *Forgive Me Father*, he confessed his sins ("I'm a homo and I'm going to hell") to a priest (the very brawny and beary Arpod Miklos), who committed a few sins on and inside of him—in the confessional. But *Bangin' Black Boyz 'n' Bootz* was the across-the-board fave: his Timberlands were literally knocked off his feet by the very well endowed Chad Hunt, who attempted to reconstruct BuTay's rectum by violently banging him up against a sanding table, hung over a stepladder and on the roof of a pile driver, as BuTay begged for both mercy *and* more. Their ferocious fuckfest (and its cum-gushing climax) deservedly won the GayVN Award for Best Couple.

BuTay didn't make the bulk of his green on the screen, though. He appeared at gay clubs and public events (from the White Party circuit to the Folsom Street Fair) where he'd autograph copies of his DVDs; in two instances caught on film, he signed one fan's chest and another's dick. He refused to dance or strip for cash; the thought of doing either made him feel...dirty. But he offered his services to a very select clientele as an escort. Men in the sex industry have adopted that title when in reality they are nothing but prostitutes, but BuTay actually escorted his callers to banquets, concerts and conferences (the married "straight" men got a kick out of introducing him as their "boyfriend," "assistant," and in one instance, "son"). His ad—which ran in *A Man's Man*, a tasteful flesh rag that caters to the wealthy, for two years—specifically stated that "sex is not a part of the package," although he would sleep in the same bed and sometimes allowed some intimate play (massage, rimming, frottage, blow jobs, mutual jerk-off), depending on the man (i.e., if they didn't totally gross him out, which was most of the time). He was paid $1,000–$1,500 for a night and $3,000–$5,000 for a weekend, *not* including first-class travel (be it on a commercial airline, their private jet or an Acela express train), ground transportation (his preference: black stretch limos), meals (an Apple marketing VP in Simi Valley hired food and wine connoisseur Ted Allen of "Queer Eye for the Straight Guy" to prepare a romantic dinner, midnight snack and breakfast for two), and "miscellaneous" (such as a clothing allowance for the appropriate wardrobe, be it a tux, a linen suit, silk pajamas, tennis wear, golf gear, even Speedos and sandals for the beach). Everyone was more than generous, but some were *really* big spenders. A forensic biologist in Reston took him on a five-day cruise to the Bahamas, where they stayed for two nights and three days at the swanky JW Marriott (BuTay couldn't get over the giant, crystal chandeliers and the gold-embossed doorknobs, handles and faucets). A Broadway producer treated him to a two-week excursion to Sydney, Amsterdam and Munich. He received $15,000 in cash and gifts (including a custom-made eel-skin coat and a forty-two-inch plasma screen television) from a cardiologist in Portland.

An entertainment lawyer in Beverly Hills sent him a Mercedes; one of *his* clients, a semicloseted Oscar-winning actor, did the same (he sold them both).

Of course, there were a few extraordinary cases where he did more than just show up. He participated in a celebrity date auction sponsored by COLT Men to benefit the pediatric AIDS ward at Los Angeles Memorial Hospital. He was "won" by Stefan and Eduardo Franz-Lopez, a professional bodybuilding international (Latvian and Ecuadorian) couple. He didn't know if the wild evening (very passionate sex on the beach, by a fire, under the moonlight) they spent together was worth the $7,650 they bid, but it was for him (it was his first—and still his best—*ménage à trois*). He earned $4,000 as a model for a Tom of Finland exhibit in San Francisco, where several of the artist's works were brought to life. He was captured being fucked in a locker room by one white man while another looked on. As BuTay stood with both his head and dick positioned to the left and arched upward, Baron was seated behind him with his dick halfway up inside BuTay, focusing on the ass while clutching BuTay around the torso with his right arm and squeezing a tube of what was marked Vaseline (it was actually toothpaste) with his left. The shoot was supposed to take less than an hour but dragged on for close to two. An exact replica of the drawing was needed (one detail was changed: it wasn't done bareback) and something was always in the wrong position: BuTay's ass, Baron's dick, BuTay's neck, Baron's left arm, BuTay's right shoulder, Baron's hair, BuTay's right elbow, Baron's left eye, BuTay's nose, Baron's left thumb, BuTay's right pinky, Baron's shorts (which were pulled down between his waist and knees). While it was supposed to *look* like they were fucking they weren't *supposed* to be fucking, and BuTay and Baron kept messing up the shot because it was feeling so good. Getting in was no problem; getting in and remaining completely still was. Baron was expected to get excited but not *too* excited, and it was *hard* for him (his dick) not to—and it was *hard* for BuTay (his ass) not to, too. Even if Baron moved his dick just a quarter inch, BuTay couldn't help but react and move his ass along (it also impressed BuTay that Baron could hold an erection for much of that time). BuTay also found it hard not to stick out his tongue, unpurse and lick his lips and hold his dick in check. Just when the photographer was about to lose the few strands of hair on his head, they finally nailed it—and then Baron went on to nail *it*. BuTay shot his own load, as did Kristoff, the voyeur, who remarked: "That was the best almost fuck I've ever seen in my life."

And let's not forget the well-known televangelist in Fort Lauderdale, who threw a costume party in which two lucky guests won a raffle to participate in a foursome—while the other eight guests watched. Clips can be found on ForbiddenVideos and XTube, with BuTay by a pool sucking off Jason Vorhees, being sucked off by Captain Hook, and getting fucked by Predator. The nine-hour fiesta, which included a buffet where the Green Lantern, Spider-Man, Batman and Robin, Pinhead, the Lone Ranger, Freddy Krueger and the Grinch doused him with soy and duck sauce and ate sushi off of him, brought him a hefty $30,000.

Evan was having fun. Lots of fun. Maybe *too* much fun. He never imagined being a part of the Triple X club and at times still couldn't believe that he was. He accepted that, at this time in his life, he was fucking for a living and there was nothing inherently wrong with that. It was easy money—he could shoot a scene a day (more like three to five hours) and make enough to cover all his bills for several months. He loved to fuck, loved to *be* fucked, so if someone wanted to shell out thousands of dollars a pop for him to get popped, why not? He paid off his student loans and became a homeowner at twenty-three, a power move that made his parents proud. He visited countries and met people he probably never would have. And his time was his own—he could devote days, sometimes an entire month, to writing the Great American Novel he'd been carrying around since he was twelve. He didn't have to punch a time clock or ask permission to take a break. He was his own boss; others had to work around his schedule—if he chose to have one.

He knew that, one day, there'd be no more gravy for the mashed potatoes—but was somewhat taken aback by the reason why.

There's an unwritten but understood rule Black actors operate under in gay porn: *Once you go Black you can never come back*. White actors can fuck and be fucked by every color of the rainbow on film but Black men usually have to choose a side. This is why you will probably never see a Matthew Rush (yeah, he's a Negro), Jay Black, Dred Scott or Simon Cox paired up with someone who doesn't have a tan courtesy of the sun or a salon (that includes your Latinos Blancos). You can start out on the Blackhand side and venture over (uh, what colored man *doesn't* want to be with a white boy?), but once you cross that white line, you fall out of flavor. You're no longer "exclusive." You are no longer "one of ours," as BuTay heard more than one white man say to him.

His membership in the Snow Patrol was revoked (and immediately passed on to Deisel Washington) with the release of *BuTay-Liscious*, his Full Moons debut. His contract was up with Good Ol' Boy and, while Jess pushed to extend it for another eight films, he wasn't interested (they did issue one last title—*Black Puddin: BuTay's Best*). After being smothered by white men for

THE LAST PICTURE. SHOW.

three years, he wished to get Black to his roots. He took a *lot* of flack from folk, Black gay folk especially, in and outside the industry, working for a company with such a "questionable" name, for *only* getting fucked by white men onscreen, and for being a snow queen (which was totally untrue; Bubba was his very first white man, and he always said the only way he'd sleep with one was if he were paid to). He had never really cared about what others thought, but being branded a traitor to the race—a spook, Mandingo, house nigger—by his own bothered him. It also ruined his love life: while marriage proposals from white men presented themselves weekly, the brothers weren't calling at all, except those who wished to brag they bagged a porn star (he could smell 'em a mile away). Even some of the cuties at Full Moons who had become friends threw him shade.

BuTay could have "retired." Between the films, photo shoots, public appearances, gifts and escort service, he'd clocked nearly a half million, most of it undeclared and sitting in various stocks, money market CDs, high-yield savings and checking accounts (he received sound financial tips from an investment banker who waived his consulting fee after BuTay waved his ass in his face and up on his dick for three hours; it was one of the few times BuTay had sex with a Black man during that whiteout period). But he felt...not obligated, not indebted, perhaps *grateful* to EJ. The man was the first to offer to put him in pictures, gave him his first big break (indirectly), and remained a close friend and confidant after he left to become part of the Good Ol' Boy family, advising him on what moves to take to make the most of his first fourteen minutes of fame.

So, to take ahold of his own image (and as sort of a quid pro quo), BuTay joined Full Moons as a contracted star player. Truth be told, BuTay was actually coming to EJ's rescue: after releasing a string of moderate successes, Full Moons was on the brink of bankruptcy. EJ needed new blood to pump new life into the company and pairing some of his somewhat-popular performers with the enormously popular BuTay could do just that. BuTay's salary dropped considerably (from $12,500 to $2,500) and the escort service dried up (the white men no longer wanted to pay for the privilege) but he didn't mind; he was, in a sense, coming back home, and his peace of mind and happiness were more important than money. While there was some initial resistance to his addition to the roster (a few refused to work with him, and one actor, Masta Ace, snapped on him to his face: "The white boys don't want yo' azz no mo', so you come to us, huh?"), that changed once they saw how uninhibited and insatiable he was (he had been storing up the *real* freakiness for some time and was finally able to let it all out). Pretty soon the other actors were jockeying for position to be next in line, including Masta Ace—and so were the "down low" hip-hop artists, R&B singers and professional ball players, who usually requested his cumpany after a concert, awards show or game. BuTay purchased a special cell just for them, their reps or their boiz to call, clocking several G's per appointment (after a few tried to use their own ice as payment, he required the funds be wired into a special account or the cash be placed in his hands before the do went down). He was also the "headliner" (he bobbed on at least a dozen knobs) at FreakOut, a midweek sexcursion for closeted Black male celebs (to keep gossip hounds like Wendy Williams at bay, the dates and city are switched each year).

So he was still BuTay, but was also affectionately referred to as EOA (Equal Opportunity Azz) by the Children, for just about every color under the sun, moon and stars had had him (on film, anyway). His FM catalog includes: *Rican Rump Shakers* (the ravenous Ricky Martinez pulverized him in the last car of a northbound #1 train on an early Sunday morning); *Dominican*

Dick Down (the "J" Crew—Jonathan, Jaime, Jiminez, Jermaine and Joey—jumped his ass as part of an initiation, then took turns jumping *in* his ass)*;* the *My _____ Guy* trilogy, in which three fans were selected by BuTay to be his costar (the *Jamaican* was Rowdy Boi; the *Brazilian,* Mighty Manuel Montez and the *Arabian,* Kaseem the Dream who, as the DVD cover proclaimed, "knows how to make BuTay scream!"); *My Chocolate Fortune Cookie* (with the delectable Brandon Lee showing BuTay how to prepare and *do* the chop suey)*; Cowboyz & Indians* (Chief Beef, a hulking six-foot, two hundred-forty-pound Navaho with a braided ponytail that reached his waist, lassoed BuTay round the waist—and up the ass); and the TLA Video #1 hits *Two Gays Can Play That Game* (in which the studio's first white actors— identical twin brothers Kain and Able—played the sex switch on and double teamed BuTay; they earned a GayVN nod for Best Threesome) and *Workin' It Out*, a tribute to the infamous *Black Workout* series of the late eighties/early nineties (and, for those in the know, the tawdry *h*enanigans at the New York Sports Club in Harlem), which brought Full Moons seven GayVN nominations—Best Director (EJ), Best Actor (BuTay), Best Duo (BuTay and Francois Sagat), Best Orgy (BuTay, Supreme, Tiger Tyson, Sexcyone, Eddie Diaz and Shorty J), Best Screenplay (Henry "The Head" Howdini and BuTay), Best Music (openly gay hip-hop artists Tori Fixx and Shorty Roc), and Best Ethnic-Themed Video (yes, a bone thrown to the "minority" flicks that usually find themselves shut out of the other categories). It only took the latter category (the first winner that didn't feature white actors in the cast), but the recognition was a vindication for EJ, who found himself mentioned in the same sentences as power-house porn director/moguls Chi Chi LaRue, Michael Lucas and Bruce Cam and invited to give insight as an "expert" in the trade publications and at porn conventions. In some quarters, Full

Moons was no longer dismissed as just another "urban" (read: Black/Latino/Blatino) studio, á la CoCoBoyz, Latino Fan Club, and StreetLife.

He had the profits, he had the profile, he finally had the respect. But there was still one thing EJ wanted.

"EJ, no." Evan pushed him back. EJ attempted to kiss him. They were alone in the office on this particular night.

EJ leaned forward; they were nose to nose. "Evan, please. I…I have wanted you for so long."

"I know."

"No, you don't know. It's not about fucking you. It's about making love to you."

Evan recalled their discussion about mixing biz and pleasure. "We work together. We're friends. It would ruin both relationships."

"But I love you."

Evan's eyes widened. "You…do?"

"Yes, I do. I always have. And I am in love with you."

"You are?"

"Yes."

Uh-oh. Evan could tell by the look in EJ's eyes that he was serious. "I…love you too, EJ, but…not that way."

EJ stepped back, looking down, defeated.

Evan reached out for him. EJ pulled away.

And he continued pulling farther away. It was never easy for EJ, watching Evan being fucked by so many others, and it certainly didn't get any easier after disclosing his feelings and being rejected. Now he was *humiliated* and had to continue directing the man he loved and was in love with being fucked by others. Before it was frustrating; now it was painful, and it pained Evan to see the pain EJ was going through. But what could he do? EJ became indifferent; he soon addressed Evan only as BuTay and would only discuss business with him.

Things became surprisingly less tense between them when Evan and Kayo (birth name Tracy Armond Murrell) fell in love. EJ "discovered" Kayo dancing as a go-go boy at Escuelita. He was one of those cornbread-fed boys ("from the 'ham") who ventured to the Big Apple to make it big. Tall, thick and torn (not ripped). Rich brown skin. Doe-eyed. Bushy eyebrows. Square jaw. A smile brighter than a neon sign.

Yup, one look and he K.O.'s you (EJ gave him the perfect stage name). As the artist once again known as Prince sang: *You sex-y motherfucker*.

When Kayo cruised (he didn't have a bop, strut or swagger, yet it was just as masculine but much more regal) into the office, and his and BuTay's eyes met...*WHAM!!!* It was a first-sight thing. As they were introduced, they shook hands and neither wanted to let go. As they made small talk on the love seat, Kayo pulled BuTay onto his left thigh; BuTay ran his fingers through his dark brown locks. They rehearsed their kissing scene at least a dozen times—and that was the *only* scene they rehearsed. When the cameras rolled and Kayo placed his arms around BuTay's waist, they *gazed* into each other's eyes and *kissed*. And when BuTay eased his azz down on Kayo's dick and they became *one*...everyone—the cameraman, the grip guy, the lighting director, the script guy and the fluff boy (whose services weren't needed at all)—could clearly see they were *not* acting. And when they, as Kayo would later describe it, "caught some heaven"...yes, the earth tilted off its axis for a second or two, it was that seismic and powerful. But everyone, including BuTay, was shocked when EJ didn't yell cut. He just let them do their thing. EJ was still love struck, but he wasn't stupid. He'd filmed several hundred scenes over a decade and had never seen such chemistry. This wasn't something you could cajole, coerce or create; it just *was*. He was witnessing magic; they were a perfect match. He saw the bottom line: the dollar sign.

So, as BuTay and Kayo reprised that love scene at BuTay's place that night, EJ plotted how to exploit their pairing to the fullest. The dynamic duo made four flicks together: *A Love for All Times* (which presented them in three different eras—the Harlem Renaissance, the disco years and the high-top fade nineties—finding each other and falling in love); *Fed Sex* (yes, Kayo delivered a package BuTay *loved* receiving); *Same Script, Different Ass* (Kayo did the same scene three times but saved the very best bootay for last); and the #1 fan fave, *Fruit Salad* (in which Kayo ate orange slices, chocolate covered cherries, blue-berry jam and grapes out of BuTay's azz)—and became the new joint face of Full Moons. They were inseparable; you didn't see one without the other. Twenty-four hours after meeting, Kayo packed up his duffel and moved out of the one-bedroom apart-ment in Rego Park, Queens, he was sharing with three room-mates (he had the sofa on odd nights, the floor on even), and into BuTay's two-bedroom co-op in Fort Greene, Brooklyn. BuTay stopped ordering from San Cho's Chinese Palace, the corner deli and Junior's every other day; Kayo whipped up meals that were filling, nutritious and tasty. Kayo encouraged BuTay to write more; BuTay encouraged Kayo to enroll in chef school. They attended Black Gay Prides in New York, Detroit, Philly, Boston, Miami and Oakland, where they were feted as the new Bobby and Flex-Deon Blake. They vacationed in Hawaii, spent Thanks-giving with Kayo's grandmother in Birmingham and visited BuTay's cousin and his partner in Charlotte for Christmas. They celebrated New Year's in Times Square, probably the only Black men kissing for close to an hour (with all those stupefyingly drunk people, no one seemed to notice). Kayo threw BuTay a surprise birthday party during Martin Luther King weekend in Atlanta. They had front-row seats for Oleta Adams at B.B. King's on Valentine's Day.

Then Kayo was killed a week later in a hit-and-run accident in Harlem. The driver, who was followed home by an eyewitness, was cited just one month earlier for driving while intoxicated, his sixth DUI citation in two years. It was because of this history (and the promise from the DA that second-degree murder charges would be sought) that the driver entered a guilty plea to voluntary vehicular manslaughter and leaving the scene of an accident. He'd eventually be sentenced to twelve years in jail and three years probation.

Evan was *devastated*. He had to identify Tracy at the morgue. He sobbed as the coroner pulled back the sheet revealing Tracy's scarred face and mangled upper body and didn't stop weeping for an entire day. Then he stood awake for another entire day, holding and smelling all of Tracy's possessions. Then he slept for an entire day. Then he became angry. And angrier. And *angrier*. Tracy was his first love, his *only* love—he'd never felt that way about anyone. Not only had he never known love like that before, he never knew that kind of love existed. He'd given up hope of finding THE ONE long before he was in the game. He didn't believe in "soul mates"—until Tracy. They fell into each other's eyes, lips, arms and lives as if they'd always been waiting for this. And Tracy was only in Evan's life for eleven months. *Eleven months. Fuck* all that "look-on-the-bright-side" bullshit: *You two were lucky to have found each other when you did. Be glad you had what you had and shared what you did. In this business, most people fly solo, and some would kill to experience what you had with him.* Evan *wasn't* thankful for what he had with Tracy, because it wasn't enough. They deserved to be together and they deserved more than what they had had.

The universe couldn't give them a year, *one* lousy fucking year? Instead of being in mourning, Evan was enraged.

EJ wasn't grieving, either. Just a week after Kayo's death, he released a *Best of* compilation that could only be downloaded online. The extras included "bloopers" (fumbled lines), "home movies" (clips of Kayo at the office and appearing at different erotica events), and Kayo's audition, in which he rubbed his body down with oil, jerked off and, on a dare, let EJ fuck him with his tongue, then his fingers, then his dick. As too many of Full Moons' models were aware, EJ had the very bad habit of slipping a mickey in the drink of a newbie. It wouldn't knock them out, just lessen their defenses, so he could "seduce" them into doing things they wouldn't normally do. Kayo claimed to be a total top but given his ass (while BuTay had an upper case *B:* Basketballs, Kayo had an upper case *P:* Plump and Protruding) and his six-month stint as an escort when he first arrived in New York (his former profile on www.rentboy.com identified him as "99% top"), the chance that someone *hadn't* been up in it was slim.

EJ was taking credit for being that someone. Anyone logging on to the Full Moons website was greeted with the banner: *Watch Kayo Get Krunked in His Trunk for the First Time!* Evan couldn't believe that EJ could be so tacky and classless, not to mention sneaky: one night many years ago when they were both a little tipsy, EJ disclosed that he had a complex about coming up short in the crotch (one would think hanging around so many Black and Latino men would make that hang-up worse). This explained why Kayo yelped with delight when the ass was tossed and the fingers probed him but could barely be heard *breathing* while being fucked. And those moans and groans? They were from *other* films he'd done (BuTay would know; he had costarred in them *and* shared a bed with the man). Kayo was knocked out from boredom, just didn't feel a thing, or both. To portray himself as a good lover, EJ had to doctor the video's soundtrack (naturally, there are no shots of his dick, just him trying to bump and grind away to no avail, then a rather unimpressive sperm spritz on Kayo's ass).

BuTay stormed into the office. "What the hell do you think you're doing?"

EJ was seated at his desk. He didn't look up from what he was reading. "What do you mean?"

"Don't you think it's too soon to put something like that out?"

"No, I don't."

"Well, it is"

"Don't tell me how to run my business."

"*Your* business? Who do you think helped build this business?"

"*Helped* build. I'm glad you know it."

"The least you could've done is let *me* know. I shouldn't have to find out about it elsewhere."

"You were his boyfriend, not his agent."

"What is your problem?"

"I don't have one."

"Why are you being nasty?"

"I'm not. I'm just being realistic."

"If *that* was the case, you wouldn't have embarrassed yourself like that."

"I haven't."

"You don't think so?"

"I know so."

"You obviously haven't been cruising the blogosphere. You're a laughing stock."

"Like I care what they think. They didn't purchase three thousand copies of the collection in three days. If anything, they're giving me free publicity blogging about it."

"This is not good publicity, EJ. Only a desperate, despicable man would release such crap, *and* put himself in it. You're fooling yourself."

"No, *you* are."

"*Oh?* And what am I fooling myself about?"

"About how you feel."

"About what?"

"You know."

Evan scoffed. "Why are you so fucking bitter?"

"Bitter? About what?"

"About us *not* being an us."

"Don't flatter yourself, BuTay."

"My *name* is *Evan*."

"*My* name suits you best. And you've proven me right by showing the world that what you sit on—and *who* you sit on—makes it your most appealing attribute."

"*Fuck you, EJ.*"

"You had your chance. Now, please leave, I have work to do. And make sure you're here tomorrow morning at six."

"What? What the hell for?"

"Because someone has to fill in for your boyfriend on the shoot."

Evan heaved. "First, I am just getting back from Birmingham—"

"Yet you had the energy to come over and berate me."

"*Secondly*, I am not ready to go back to work."

"You have no choice."

"Say what?"

"You are still under contract. You don't get to choose what

films you do; *I* make that decision." He smiled. "Besides, I'm sure he'd want you to carry on for him."

Evan was flabbergasted. "You said I could have the rest of the month off."

"Six A.M. Sharp. Please." He turned back to the paperwork.

BuTay read his contract, and there it was in black and white: clause 23/a did in fact say that if he didn't follow the boss's orders, he could be sued for breach of contract; any monies owed him by the studio would be used not only to pay other actors for the work he wouldn't do but to cover EJ's legal fees as well. EJ never had a reason to invoke the clause before; even when they weren't getting along, he always put the image and reputation of Full Moons way above being spiteful. Not any longer.

BuTay arrived at the office at 5:59 A.M.

He was contractually bound to do three more films after filling in for Kayo in *Hot Sauce* (it wasn't used as a condiment). He was slammed by Lil' Walter, who was no more than five feet tall but had one humongous stick. BuTay's heart wasn't in it. Neither was his ass. But he still gave it "that old college try" (one of EJ's standard lines when he wasn't getting what he wanted out of an actor) and came through—and *came*.

He managed to cum on the next film—*Fat Is Where It's At*—despite being paired with gentlemen who could moon-light as sumo wrestlers. EJ took great glee in watching BuTay being mashed into the mattress by the rotund Latino and getting thrown around as if he were a rag doll by the beyond-bear white boy. The brother was also a blob, but at least he was agile and had good coordination for a man his size.

And he even came during *Gangstas & Goths*, EJ's disastrous rip-off of *Ruffnecks & Rednecks*—but it wasn't easy. During the entire shoot, he was mentally reciting the Lord's Prayer, calling on the angels to protect him from any unholy spirits that surrounded his partner, who looked like one of the devil's disciples: skin white as milk decorated with black eyeliner and black lipstick; black Doc Martens, black stonewashed jeans, black mock and a black cape; and wavy black hair styled in the shape of horns. That's right, *horns*. But the tongue piercing saved the day (his chin, both lips, both nostrils, both ears, both eyebrows and his navel were also clipped). BuTay had never been kissed or tasted by a man with one—and it turned him *on*. And Damien (his *given* name; BuTay just knew he'd find 666 engraved on him somewhere) enjoyed eating ass more than fucking it—he spent ten minutes doing the former rather splendidly, fifteen on the latter with very lackluster results, then returned to the former for another twenty-five thrilling minutes. Since BuTay was lying on his belly, he didn't have to look at Damien's frightening face. Their fountains spouted at the same time.

But BuTay wouldn't be cumming today. EJ was hell-bent on sticking it to him one more time, showing neither compassion nor sorrow over Kayo's death or sympathy for BuTay's loss. Placing him in projects he knew would fuck with him—or fuck him over. Now, this. EJ's final chance to humiliate BuTay. And once again, someone else would be doing the dirty work. BuTay didn't like his own sperm being on his body and only tolerated it being dumped on his back or legs or ass or chest by others (it's expected in the porn trade). But this...*this* was just a half step away from pissing in somebody's face.

Big hunched up. He huffed. He hollered, "I'm cummin', yo," seven or eight times (*then cum already, motherfucker*). He aimed. He fired.

He fell.

BuTay had pushed him off—and that was no easy feat. Big

was a hulky dude, but BuTay managed to unpin his left leg.

As his dick ejaculated onto the floor, Big looked up, incredulous. "*What the fuck, yo?*"

BuTay didn't answer. He slid off the bed, swooped up his clothes and barreled down the bunker steps, everyone watching in shock.

EJ was right behind him. He grabbed BuTay's left arm. "Where do you think you're going?"

BuTay snatched it away. "*Get* your fuckin' hands off me."

"You are not going to fuck this up for me."

"Hmph, I just did." He began putting on his clothes.

"You better get your black ass back up there."

"Oh. My *Black* ass? Careful, the red is starting to show on your neck."

"Don't try that race card crap with me."

"You're the one holding—and *dealing*—from that deck."

"I've just about had it with you."

"Oh? And what are you going to do *with* me, Massa?"

"I'm not your Massa. But you have been pimping yourself out as a slave to masters for some time."

BuTay rolled his eyes. "Uh-huh."

"What's the line you use? 'It's my job.' You've been using porn as an excuse to fulfill your desire of being possessed by us. But let a white man who doesn't want to fuck you on camera or pay you for it express genuine interest, and you run in the other direction..."

"Who the fuck are you, Dr. Frances Cress Welsing? You just can't let it go, can you? I don't want your ass. I *never* wanted your ass. And why *would* I want your ass? But if a Negro *doesn't* want your ass, something's *got* to be wrong with him, right? And you don't think you're suffering from post-traumatic slave/master syndrome?"

EJ poked at BuTay's chest. "I expect you to fulfill your contractual obligations."

"I already have."

"I don't know what makes you think you're so special. We all have to do things in this life we may not want to."

"I do not like my face being used as a toilet. But then, you already knew that."

"Either you get back up there, or I will haul your ass into court."

"For what? Refusing to be assaulted by sperm?"

"And I'll let the IRS know about your under-the-table gigs."

"Let's not go there. You forget, I managed this bitch for a year. Who do you think I learned the shit from? They'll be making a deal with *me* to get to *you*."

EJ was stung but not stuck. He grinned. "*And*, I'll make sure your secret is revealed. I'm sure your mother and father would *love* to get a collection of your greatest hits on DVD."

Blackmail? How appropriate. But BuTay couldn't be worried about it, and he wasn't. He was tired. Tired of fighting. Tired of feeling helpless. Tired of feeling alone. Tired of feeling lonely. He was disgusted with the whole thing and disgusted with himself. He wanted his man back. He wanted his body back; it hadn't belonged to him in years, and he'd lost a piece of himself every time he gave someone a piece. He wanted to be able to tell his parents what he did for a living ("public relations" had been the usual line—and it wasn't altogether untrue). He wanted to work on that Great American Novel, which he hadn't written a single line of since becoming an actor. He wanted his life back. And if freedom meant that being a video ho' would come to light, bring it.

Of course, he couldn't let EJ think that would scare him. So he hit him *way* below the belt. "Secret? You mean, like having a four-inch dick and drugging others so you can get your pebble off?"

EJ *fumed*; the red was really showing on his neck now. *"You stupid nigger!"*

There was a unified, audible gasp from the gallery upstairs. BuTay thought: *Was this lily-white crew genuinely shocked that he had called me such a vulgar name—or were they genuinely shocked that he had called me such a vulgar name to my face?* BuTay knew the epithet—or something like it—would spew from his mouth sooner or later. It may no longer be fashionable or acceptable for white folks to just come right out and call a Black person a nigger, but that didn't mean they've stopped. Some forget that it is the twenty-first century and let it rip (like Michael Richards and Dog the Bounty Hunter). But most dance around it—and it always comes down to you not knowing your place. It wasn't until he had the gall to reject a white man's advances or challenge his paternalistic colonial attitude—that buying his time meant that they were buying *him*—that BuTay went from being lovely, gorgeous, alluring, a dream/fantasy come true and all that to porch monkey, darkie, mud boy, jigaboo, Magilla Gorilla and the Big N.

BuTay knew where it came from, that it demonstrated just how much contempt they had for Black men (if not all Black people), and that he was and would have to be the bigger person and ignore their ignorance. EJ was no different. *He* may have thought he was a different kind of white man (don't they all think that?), but he was still white. Once again, BuTay would have to rise above it and rise above him. But this time, because he *knew* the white man...BuTay really wanted to haul off and punch the shit out of him.

But Big beat him to it.

Wrapped in a white towel, Big happened to be standing

just a few feet behind EJ. He snatched EJ up by the back of his collar, swung him around and bopped him in the left cheek (the crunch made everyone flinch, including BuTay). EJ soared into the air and flew over what used to be Evan's desk and into the file cabinet.

Paralyzed with fascination (or was it fear?), the crew stood in silence, mouths agape.

"*Who you callin' nigger, cracker?*" Big bellowed at EJ, who was knocked the fuck out. He turned to BuTay. "Man, ya shoulda told me that ain't yo' thang. This mo'-fo' said you liked gettin' shot in the face. No foul. You cool?"

Hmm...as many times as EJ hoped to lay my ass out behind that desk...

BuTay smiled at Big. "Yeah. Now I am."

ABOUT THE AUTHORS

SHANE ALLISON is the editor of *Hot Cops, Backdraft, College Boys, Homo Thugs, Hard Working Men* and *Black Fire*. His stories have graced the pages of several Cleis Press anthologies, including four lustful editions of *Best Gay Erotica*. His first book of poems, *Slut Machine,* is out from Rebel Satori Press.

ERIC KARL ANDERSON is author of the novel *Enough* and has published work in various publications, among them *The Ontario Review*, Blithe House Quarterly, *Ganymede*, Velvet Mafia, and the anthologies *From Boys to Men* and *Between Men 2*.

JONATHAN ASCHE's work has appeared in numerous anthologies, including *Rough Trade* and *Muscle Men*. He is also the author of the erotic novels *Mindjacker* and *Moneyshots* and the short-story collection *Kept Men*. He lives in Atlanta with his husband, Tomé.

DANIEL ALLEN COX (danielallencox.com) is the author of the novel *Shuck*, shortlisted for a Lambda Literary Award and a ReLit Award, as well as the novel *Krakow Melt*. Daniel writes the column "Fingerprinted" for *Xtra* and lives in Montreal.

MARTIN DELACROIX (martindelacroix.wordpress.com) writes novels, novellas and short fiction. His stories have appeared in more than a dozen erotic anthologies. He has published two novellas, *Maui* and *Love Quest*. He lives with his partner, Greg, on a barrier island on Florida's Gulf Coast.

RAWLEY GRAU, originally from Baltimore, has lived in Slovenia since 2001. Translations from Slovenian include Boris Pintar's short-prose collection *Family Parables* and Vlado Zabot's novel *The Succubus* (translated with Nikolai Jeffs). He is preparing a translation from Russian of Evgeny Baratynsky's poems.

JAMES EARL HARDY is the author of the best-selling *B-Boy Blues* series. His novella, "Is It Still Jood to Ya?" is featured in *Visible Lives: Three Stories in Tribute to E. Lynn Harris*. His one-man show about Tiger Tyson, "Confessions of a Homo Thug Porn Star," won the Downtown Urban Theater Festival's 2010 Best Short Prize. He lives in New York.

SHAUN LEVIN (shaunlevin.com) is the author, most recently, of *Snapshots of The Boy*. His other books include *Seven Sweet Things* and *A Year of Two Summers*. He is the founding editor of *Chroma*, a queer literary and arts journal.

JEFF MANN has published two books of poetry, *Bones Washed with Wine* and *On the Tongue*; a collection of memoir and poetry, *Loving Mountains, Loving Men*; a book of essays, *Edge* and a volume of short fiction, *A History of Barbed Wire*, winner of a Lambda Literary Award.

JOHNNY MURDOC (johnnymurdoc.com) lives in St. Louis with his partner of eight years. His interests include porn, comics and copyright law. Johnny's own erotic comic is *Crash Course*. He writes essays for edenfantasys.com/sexis/, self-publishes the zine *Blowjob*, and was previously published in *Skater Boys*.

TONY PIKE's erotic fiction has previously appeared in *Zipper* and *Vulcan* magazines in the U.K. and in the anthologies *Dorm Porn II* and *Boy Crazy*. He is looking forward to the publication of his first erotic novel, *Summer Term Boys*.

BORIS PINTAR, born in Slovenia in 1964, is the author of the novel *Don't Kill Anyone, I Love You*, published in English under the pseudonym Gojmir Polajnar; of two short-prose collections, including *Family Parables* and of a book of essays on the Slovene theater.

THOMAS REES (nightmaresextape.blogspot.com), Ted to his friends, has had work published in *The Swan's Rag* and *TRY Magazine*, as well as a collaborative work with Brooklyn-based visual artist Camilla Padgitt-Coles in the inaugural issue of *Perfect Wave*. He is working on a collection of fiction and lives in Oakland.

DOMINIC SANTI (dominicsanti@yahoo.com) is a former technical editor turned rogue whose stories have appeared in dozens of publications, including several volumes of *Best Gay Erotica*. Santi's latest solo book is the German collection *Buddy Action*. Future plans include more dirty short stories and an even dirtier historical novel.

SIMON SHEPPARD (simonsheppard.com) is making his eighteenth appearance in the *Best Gay Erotica* series. He edited the Lambda Award–winning *Homosex: Sixty Years of Gay Erotica* and *Leathermen;* wrote *In Deep: Erotic Stories; Kinkorama; Sex Parties 101; Hotter Than Hell* and *Sodomy!* and has been published in more than three hundred anthologies.

NATTY SOLTESZ (nattysoltesz.com) cowrote the 2009 porn film *Dad Takes a Fishing Trip* with director Joe Gage and is a faithful contributor to *Handjobs* and the Nifty Erotic Stories Archive. His first novel, *Backwoods*, is forthcoming. He lives in Pittsburgh with his boo.

ROB WOLFSHAM (wolfshammy.com) is a twenty-four-year-old West Texas escapee. He has no idea where he'll be by the time you read this. His work appears in numerous anthologies, including *Beautiful Boys, Hard Working Men, Muscle Men* and *Best Gay Erotica 2010*.

ABOUT THE EDITORS

KEVIN KILLIAN, one of the original "New Narrative" writers of the 1980s, is the author of many books of prose and poetry, including three novels *(Shy, Arctic Summer, Spreadeagle)* and three collections of short stories, the most recent of which, *Impossible Princess* (City Lights Books, 2009), won the 2010 Lambda Literary Award for Gay Erotica. Killian's most recent book is *The Kenning Anthology of Poets Theater, 1945-1985* (Kenning Editions, 2010), coedited with David Brazil; next up, a second volume of his popular *Selected Amazon Reviews* is expected this winter. Born on Long Island, he lives in San Francisco.

RICHARD LABONTÉ (tattyhill@gmail.com) was a gay bookseller for twenty years, has written book reviews for more than thirty years, has edited about thirty (mostly erotic) gay anthologies for Cleis Press and Arsenal Pulp Press and spends his weekends as a kitchen assistant preparing lunches and dinners for as many as sixty people. He lives on beautiful Bowen Island, a short ferry ride from Vancouver, with husband Asa Dean Liles and dog Zak. Several editions of the *Best Gay Erotica* series, which he has edited since 1996, have been Lambda Literary Award finalists, and two have won, as has *First Person Queer* (Arsenal Pulp), coedited with Lawrence Schimel.

More Gay Erotic Stories
from Richard Labonté

Muscle Men
Rock Hard Gay Erotica
Edited by Richard Labonté

Muscle Men is a celebration of the body beautiful, where men who look like Greek gods are worshipped for their outsized attributes. Editor Richard Labonté takes us into the erotic world of body builders and the men who desire them.
ISBN 978-1-57344-392-0 $14.95

Bears
Gay Erotic Stories
Edited by Richard Labonté

These uninhibited symbols of blue-collar butchness put all their larger-than-life attributes—hairy flesh, big bodies, and that other party-size accoutrement—to work in these close encounters of the furry kind.
ISBN 978-1-57344-321-0 $14.95

Country Boys
Wild Gay Erotica
Edited by Richard Labonté

Whether yielding to the rugged charms of that hunky ranger or skipping the farmer's daughter in favor of his accommodating son, the men of *Country Boys* unabashedly explore sizzling sex far from the city lights.
ISBN 978-1-57344-268-8 $14.95

Daddies
Gay Erotic Stories
Edited by Richard Labonté

Silver foxes. Men of a certain age. Guys with baritone voices who speak with the confidence that only maturity imparts. The characters in *Daddies* take you deep into the world of father figures and their admirers.
ISBN 978-1-57344-346-3 $14.95

Boy Crazy
Coming Out Erotica
Edited by Richard Labonté

From the never-been-kissed to the most popular twink in town, *Boy Crazy* is studded with explicit stories of red-hot hunks having steamy sex.
ISBN 978-1-57344-351-7 $14.95

Ordering is easy! Call us toll free or fax us to place your MC/VISA order.
You can also mail the order form below with payment to:
Cleis Press, 2246 Sixth St., Berkeley, CA 94710.

ORDER FORM

QTY	TITLE	PRICE
_____	_____	_____
_____	_____	_____
_____	_____	_____
_____	_____	_____
_____	_____	_____
_____	_____	_____
_____	_____	_____
_____	_____	_____

SUBTOTAL _____

SHIPPING _____

SALES TAX _____

TOTAL _____

Add $3.95 postage/handling for the first book ordered and $1.00 for each additional book. Outside North America, please contact us for shipping rates. California residents add 9.75% sales tax. Payment in U.S. dollars only.

* Free book of equal or lesser value. Shipping and applicable sales tax extra.

Cleis Press • Phone: (800) 780-2279 • Fax: 510-845-8001
orders@cleispress.com • www.cleispress.com
You'll find more great books on our website

Follow us on Twitter @cleispress • Friend/fan us on Facebook